30

RED

DRESSES

Johan Twiss

DEDICATION

To those suffering from the evils of human trafficking, my heart aches for you. I weep for you. I pray for you. And I will try to help as best as I can.

And to those wonderful organizations and souls who are fighting against this modern slavery, I say thank you. Keep up the good fight.

- 1 -
Birthday

I wonder if he will remember it's my birthday? Veata thought.

Chances were there would be no gifts and she would spend the day doing all the housework—as usual—but that did not prevent a smile from spreading across her face.

Today I am eight!

She prepared breakfast, enjoying the smells of fried eggs and curry wafting through the tiny one-room shack. The smells reminded her of her mother's cooking, bringing a tinge of sadness to the happy day. It had been two years since her parents died from cholera and she desperately missed them—struggling to keep their faces in her memory.

She was sent to live with her uncle, who spent his days gambling—that is, when he wasn't passed out, drunk, or hitting her. Still, it was her birthday and she was happy.

Veata heard a low growl from the other side of the hut and watched her uncle lazily roll off his sleeping mat. Rubbing his eyes, he sat up and grunted his disapproval at rising so early.

"Good morning, Uncle," Veata said quietly. Her special eyes saw brown, flat swirls of color slowly shifting around her uncle. He was tired and groggy, but she was thankful he was not in a bad mood.

Since the time of her first memories, Veata had always seen the colors surrounding others. Her mom had been a bright yellow, like the sun, and her dad a watery bright green, like the rice fields he worked in. Her mom had always told her she had special eyes and that hers were a gift—the ability to see the aura of others—but Veata did not know what aura meant. To her they were just colors, and all living things showed her their true colors.

Her Uncle slowly stood up, a grimace crossing his face as he arched his back to stretch. With heavy feet, he walked over to the tiny stove and scooped up one of the fried eggs Veata had cooked.

"I'm going to the city today," he announced. "You're coming with me. Clean up and get ready."

Veata froze, her face flushed with anticipation at the unexpected birthday surprise. She had spent her entire life in their small village and this would be her first trip to Phnom Penh, the capital city of Cambodia.

Her uncle's colors changed from dingy brown, to emerald green, with a shade of gray swirling around him. She'd never seen him this excited before.

The bus ride was long and uneventful, but as the city came into view, she marveled at the tall buildings, paved streets and thousands of cars.

Veata swallowed a lump in her throat. *All those people*, she thought. *They look just like the ants after I poke an anthill.*

The bus stopped in an older part of town and her uncle motioned for her to get off with him. Veata silently followed her uncle through a maze of narrow and increasingly dirty alleys. The colors of those she passed varied like a rainbow—some dazzling and bright while others were dull and dark.

After turning down a new alley, Veata nearly collided with her uncle when he came to an abrupt stop outside a weathered green door.

"Wait here!" he said sharply, waving his finger at her. "I'm going inside to take care of some business. Don't you dare move!"

Veata nodded and waited patiently in the alley, but curiosity led her to explore her surroundings. Near a pile of trash, she found two small snails. Their colors were shimmering pink and silver. With the snails in one hand, she gathered up two sticks and built a makeshift track.

"All right, little ones," she whispered, placing one snail in each lane. "Race!"

The snails crept forward. One gradually veered into the middle stick. *Oh no, he's trapped.* Veata reached down to free the snail and heard the door open behind her.

Her uncle exited with a stranger who had spiky black hair that was dyed red at the tips. The stranger handed her uncle a small stack of cash and they shook hands.

Veata tilted her head. *I've never seen Uncle smile before*, she thought as his colors exploded in dark green and violet.

"There," her uncle pointed dismissively at Veata. Looking greedily at his newfound wealth, he turned and walked away. Veata stood to follow, but the spiky-haired man grabbed her from behind, smothering her mouth with his dirty hand.

She bit the man's hand and screamed, "UNCLE! COME BACK!"

Her uncle stopped and turned around. His colors went solid gray, like cold, hard stone, and flashed dark green as he looked longingly at the money in his fist. Without a word, he turned his back on Veata a second time, and left the alley.

Veata screamed and scratched, vainly attempting to twist free as the man dragged her into the building. He threw her into a large closet and slapped her across the face.

"I'll keep hitting you until you stop screaming!" he shouted, his colors changing from dull gray to burning red and orange as he slapped her.

Each blow felt like a hammer driving Veata deeper within herself. She stopped screaming, but her mind pleaded, *Help! Uncle! Come back! Help me! Someone help me!*

But no one came.

The spiky-haired man ignored her tears. His gray colors moved sluggishly around his body as he looked down on her. He grabbed a tiny red dress from a shelf and threw it at her. Veata watched as the dress fluttered in the air, almost gliding, before falling to the dirty floor at her feet.

"Change!" the man commanded.

Veata tasted the salty tears streaming down her face, trying to push away the pain—trying to understand. An image of her mother in a yellow dress drifted into her mind.

"Mama," she sobbed as her mother smiled and extended open arms to comfort her.

"Mama. Hold me." Veata reached out to her mother, their fingers nearly touching, when a hard slap crashed against her cheek. Her mother disappeared.

"Shut up and change!"

Veata blinked rapidly, trying to bring her mother back into view, but she was gone. "No," she whimpered. "Come back, Mama."

"I told you to shut up and change," the man hissed. He reached back his hand to hit her again, but Veata quickly grabbed the dress off the floor and began changing to avoid being hit.

The man grunted, seemingly satisfied as he lowered his raised hand.

Once she dressed, the man grabbed her by the arm, led her down a hallway, and shoved her into a small room with a dozen other girls in red dresses. All of the girls looked much older to Veata, like teenagers. Some whispered to one another while others stared blankly at a maroon colored curtain against one wall.

"Stop talking and line up!" the spiky-haired man shouted.

As he walked down the line, he stopped at each girl and placed a sign over their neck. Written on the signs were numbers. Veata's read "30".

Bright lights came to life above them and Veata shielded her eyes.

"Show time," the man called. He pulled a rope that opened the velvety curtains, revealing a large glass window on the other side.

None of the girls spoke, but some began posing and twisting. Through the glare of the lights, Veata saw they were standing on a stage with men looking at them through the glass. Some of the men pointed toward her. Weak, frightened, and too hurt from the beating to fathom what was happening, she stared at the ground, paralyzed. Tears trickled down her cheeks.

Today is my eighth birthday.

- 2 -
Rain

James set down the pen and rubbed his aching hand, thankful the long line of fans had finally disappeared. The jet lag from flying into Cambodia early that morning was catching up with him. He hated flying, especially on international flights, and felt a throbbing headache building at the base of his skull.

I need a Dr. Pepper and a long nap, he thought, continuing to massage his hand.

But the hand cramp from Hades wouldn't let up after nearly five hours of signing book after book for his fans at the Momentum Bookshop in downtown Phnom Penh.

He still couldn't believe how many people showed for the signing. Upon arriving at the bookstore, the line outside the front doors wrapped around the corner of the building.

For once, I was wrong. Apparently, 'Whispers of Golgomoth' really is big in Cambodia.

He had doubted his agent's claim that a trip to Asia would prove worthwhile, but the first movie was about to be released. It had been a dud in the U.S., but projections showed it grossing quadruple overseas, especially in Asia.

His translator, a young local by the name of Munny Chey, tapped him on the shoulder.

"Are you ready to go back to your hotel?" Munny asked with a broad smile. "It is only mile to your hotel, Mr. Moore. I thought we walk and I take you on scenic tour. Show you all the best sights."

James groaned and ran a hand through his thick mop of gray hair. He'd just turned sixty last month, and felt like an old geriatric standing next to Munny, who was barely twenty and full of energy. It also didn't help that James stood a more than a foot taller than Munny, at six-foot-eight inches, making him feel like he was being accompanied by a little kid.

"I don't know," James murmured. "I just want to grab a cab and head straight to the hotel. We have two more signings tomorrow and then I head to Thailand and Hong Kong after that."

Munny shook his head and clucked his tongue. "No, no, Mr. Moore. You been sitting all day on plane and in hard store chair. Walking good for you. Good for heart," he said, thumping his chest. "Plus, cab drivers here are cuckoo. Like riding in metal death trap. No, you come follow me and I show you the best of Phnom Penh. Trust Munny Chey. He help you see."

Munny beamed another youthful smile and James rolled his eyes, letting out a soft chuckle. He couldn't help but laugh at the way Munny's name was pronounced in the Khmer language.

Money G, he help you see, he thought. *The kid sounds like a rapper straight outta Compton.*

James stood up from the chair he'd been planted in the last five hours. Pain pulsed through his arthritic knee. It was a constant reminder of an old football injury from his college days.

"Fine. We can walk," he relented, hoping his knee wouldn't swell up like a cantaloupe later that night. But his doctor had told him he needed to exercise more, not to mention lose a good eighty pounds.

After offering his thanks to the bookstore staff, James stepped outside and groaned.

The air was thick, muggy, and a stifling 102 degrees Fahrenheit with 99% humidity.

"Just imagine you're back in Dallas," he muttered to himself, sweat immediately forming along his brow. "It's just as hot here as it is back home."

But Phnom Penh was nothing like Dallas. The architecture, the sounds and even the smells were different. Spicy scents of curry and other seasonings wafted through the old streets as they passed a handful of small cafes. Though the smells were interesting, they were not what James associated with food and his stomach turned at the thought of eating the local cuisine.

But there was at least one thing that felt familiar to James—the sight and sound of hundreds of cars stuck in traffic. Oddly, he found the smell of exhaust comforting. He'd always been a bit of a gearhead, and this was a smell that he recognized and understood.

Munny pointed out various landmarks, like the Royal Palace with its ornate golden spires and immaculate garden park set against the backdrop of the river. And although James would never admit it to his young guide, the more they walked, the happier he was with the decision to skip the cab back to the hotel. It felt good to be out on a walk, even if the exertion caused him to breathe a little harder than normal.

"We go on shortcut now," Munny said with a grin. "It faster and I show you best view of Mekong River. They almost finish brand new dam up the river. Bring power to city. Very nice. Had problems with other dam built further north. Broke and flooded farms. Bad karma."

James wrinkled his brow. "Bad karma? What's that supposed to mean? Like bad luck? I didn't think that's how karma even worked."

Munny nodded. "You right, Mr. Moore. You very smart man. I start saying 'bad karma' around English tourists when I first start translating. They always ask if doing this or that bring bad karma. I joke with them and start saying it all the time. Now it like bad habit. But tourists eat it up."

Munny gave James a wink and turned down a narrow alley, escaping the main thoroughfare and the noise of the busy street. The wind picked up and dark clouds blew in overhead. A few minutes later, a light drizzle began to fall.

James wiped a mixture of water and sweat from his face, removing his glasses after his futile attempts to keep them dry. "Maybe we should head back to the main road and get a cab."

"Bah," Munny replied. "The monsoon rains come every day. Last one hour. You either soak with sweat or soak with rain. You get used to it my friend."

"We wouldn't be soaked with rain or sweat if we had taken a cab," James scoffed, becoming annoyed by the constant drizzle.

Munny only smiled. "Ah, Mr. Moore, but now you experience the real Phnom Penh."

Now that his clothes were wet and sticking to his skin, James' previous appreciation for the walking tour all but disappeared. The only thing he wanted to experience at this point was a hot shower and his hotel bed.

Grumbling to himself, James followed Munny through a maze of streets as drips of rain fell from his gray hair and ran down his neck under the collar of his blue button-up shirt. The wet clothes rubbed against his skin, chaffing with each step.

A clap of thunder shook the air and lightning danced through the sky. They turned another corner, walking onto a deserted street. James felt the wind slam into him as they came into view of the Mekong River shoreline. The view was striking as the gray clouds swirled over the wide expanse of the river. The powerful winds struck up white-capped waves that crashed against the massive dam that was still under construction. Another clap of thunder rang out, and as if on cue, the light drizzle transformed into sheets of torrential rain.

"This is bad karma! This much rain not normal!" Munny shouted over the deafening sound of water pounding the tin rooftops of nearby buildings.

"No. Really?" James shouted back sarcastically. "I thought you were *used* to this weather."

The road by the river was not paved, forcing the two men to trudge through thickening, sludgy mud. Another crack of thunder shook above them, and James felt like someone was blasting him with a fire hose from heaven. Visibility nearly disappeared, and soon the painful, hammering rain was replaced by painful, hammering hail.

"We need cover, *now!*" James shouted as the hail grew in size, golf-ball-size chunks of ice pummeling his head and shoulders.

They lifted their shirts over their heads in a poor attempt to protect themselves. Reaching the door of an old building, James started pounding. No answer. He tried to open it. Locked.

Fumbling their way down the muddy street, they turned into a narrow alley, searching for refuge. Munny pointed to a worn green door further down. James hurried toward it, but his shoe started to slip off in the mud and he tripped.

Hard chunks of ice slammed into his back as he laid face first in the brown sludge. He struggled to get up, slipping on the muddy surface, until Munny held out a hand to steady him.

Together, they trudged to the green door. James pulled on the handle. It opened.

"Thank goodness," James panted as he and Munny slogged through the door, filthy and dripping wet.

Immediately, James' senses were assaulted by the smell of body odor, stale cigarettes, and alcohol. A thick, bald man stood up from a stool in the corner of the entry room and eyed the two newcomers in annoyance before speaking in Khmer.

James looked to Munny for a translation and Munny's eyes went wide. He shook his head and whispered, "bad karma."

A puddle of muddy water collected on the floor beneath James and his one bare foot. The burly, bald man spoke again, his voice rising this time as he waited for a response.

Munny shook his head. "This is bad place, Mr. Moore. We should leave. He ask if you American. Say he take care of you, but we pay to enter. No just hide from rain for free."

"Fine. I'll pay!" James barked in irritation. He was soaking wet, covered in mud, and he could feel welts forming on his back and head from the impact of the hail. No matter the cost, he was not going back outside and into *that* storm.

James pulled out his wallet and struggled to remove a couple of soaked bills clinging together. "Here! Is this enough?" James scoffed, shoving the money toward the doorman.

"Wow, that lot of cash," Munny said in surprise. "I not believe you carry that much money. You pay him way too much. One red bill more than plenty."

The doorman eyed the bills greedily and reached out to snag them, but James pulled the wad of money back and peeled away one of the red bills.

The doorman started yelling at them, pointing at the remaining cash in James hand.

"He say you pay all money in wallet or he kick us out," Munny translated.

"What? No way!" James yelled back at the man. "You can tell this greedy little—" but James' words were cut short when the doorman produced a large handgun from his back waistband.

He waved the gun at James and reached out for the rest of the money.

"Seriously? You're robbing us?!" James shouted, pulling the wallet close to his chest. "Do you have any idea what it's like outside?"

James flared his nostrils, his temper rising out of control. He took a menacing step toward the doorman. His chest heaved up and down as he stood up to his full height, towering over the bouncer.

Munny put a hand on James' arm and pulled him back.

"What you doing? You crazy? He has gun, remember?"

"Yeah, I remember," James said through gritted teeth, slowly backing down. "But if he didn't I'd kick his can to Timbuktu! Dirty little..."

James continued to grumble under his breath as he handed the money to the bouncer. "Does this happen to you often?" James questioned Munny. "Did you bring me here on purpose to get robbed? How much do you make off this? What's your cut?"

Munny paled and nervously rubbed his hands together. "I so sorry, Mr. Moore. I never bring you to place like this on purpose. I promise. I cut no. No cutting for me. I swear. This storm crazy. It brought us here. It not normal."

James scoffed at his translator, even though he believed Munny. He knew their current situation was not *completely* Munny's fault, but he still wanted someone to blame.

The bouncer stuffed the soggy money into his pants pocket and smirked at James. He nodded for them to go through the next door into the building. He started to put his gun away, when a deep, ominous roar reverberated through the ground and up the walls.

"*What* is that?" James asked, the roar growing louder and louder—like a freight train barreling toward them.

The door to the alley began to creak and moan as water seeped underneath it. With a scowl, the burly man pushed Munny and James aside to inspect the disturbance.

As he reached to open the alley door, realization dawned on James.

The rain. The hail. The new dam on the river.

"*NO!*" he shouted.

But it was too late.

- 3 -
Candy

Veata felt dizzy under the bright lights of the stage. She was thirsty, hungry, and her face stung where she'd been slapped.

A shorter man with a thin goatee tapped on the glass in front of her. Veata looked up from the floor and saw him smiling hungrily at her. Even through the blinding lights of the stage, she saw his colors flare purple and dark blue, like the colors her uncle turned whenever he brought a woman home and kicked Veata out of the hut for a few hours.

"That one," he eagerly called, pointing at Veata. "The young one. Number 30."

Heavy footsteps marched up behind her and spiky-hair's rough hand grabbed her by the arm, squeezing tightly, as he pulled her off the stage.

He brought her down a narrow hallway and knocked on a door with a tinted window.

"Come in," a dry voice called.

Veata was shoved into the room and nearly gagged on the overpowering smell of incense burning atop a shelf on the wall. Sitting behind a desk was a new man she had not seen yet. He was heavy-set with a thin mustache and black hair slicked into a ponytail. He wore a red button-up shirt with a yellow flower print, and there was a cigarette hanging from his lips.

"Is this the new one?" the man behind the desk asked.

The guy holding her arm nodded.

The man behind the desk tilted his head to the side, looking Veata up and down, then stroked his mustache approvingly. "What's your name, child?"

Veata's jaw still hurt from where she'd been slapped, but she whispered out, "Veata."

"Veata," he said smoothly. "What a beautiful name. We will keep your name. Sometimes we change the girl's names, but we will keep yours. Come closer so I can see you better in the light."

Veata's heart beat faster. She took in the man's colors and shook her head. *So much blackness, red, and violet. So dark. So dark.*

The red, black and violet swirled around him like a mist in bad storm. She took a few steps back, but the man holding her arm yanked her forward toward the desk.

"You are young. Very young. Customers will pay extra for a girl like you—the clean ones with no diseases."

The man reached across the desk and held Veata by the chin, tilting her head side to side. "Good. Very good. You will make me money for a long time."

Releasing Veata, he took a long drag from his cigarette before squashing the embers in an ashtray. "My name is Rithisak. Your uncle sold you to me. That makes you my property. Do you understand?"

Veata's lip trembled and she shook her head.

Rithisak raised an eyebrow. "It means you do as I say. If you try to run, I will catch you. If you go to the police, they will bring you back to me. You have no more family. You have no more friends. You only have me. I will take care of you, Veata, *if* you listen and obey. Now, do you understand?"

Veata's chin quivered, and fresh tears welled in her eyes, but she nodded.

"Good little girl. Teng says a customer has already chosen you. Well done. Starting tomorrow, you will serve fifteen to twenty customers a day. Do what they ask to make them happy. If you do a good job, you will get dinner each night and *special* medicine to take away any pain. But if you're a bad little girl—"

The man's voice rose and he shook his head, his dark eyes narrowing. Veata gasped, flinching as his colors flared black and red, shifting violently like a thunderstorm.

"Good. I see you understand. You are a quick learner."

Rithisak reached across the desk and lifted Veata's hand to look at her wrist. "Teng," he growled to the spiky-haired man at her side. "Why isn't she marked yet?"

Teng shrank back at Rithisak's words and Veata wondered if he could see the stormy colors as well.

"Idiot!" Rithisak yelled. He picked up a stapler from his desk and threw it at the man, hitting him in the side of the face before he could react. "You are trying my patience, boy! If you cannot follow my simple rules, you are useless to the Sen Zi. One more mistake and I will have you beat, your mother and brother beat, and then have all of you thrown out of your apartment and into the street! Do you understand?"

Teng nodded vigorously. "Yes, Rithisak. I'm sorry. The show was about to start and I thought it best to put her on immediately. I—"

Rithisak cut him off with a sharp hand gesture. He glared at Teng and Veata watched his color swirl dark red, like blood.

"I will not tell you this again. All new girls must be tattooed before they serve any clients! Take care of it quickly so the customer is not kept waiting. Go!"

Teng gave a curt head nod and nearly yanked Veata's arm out of her socket as he pulled her out of the room. She struggled to keep up with his pace as he half-dragged her down the hallway into another room.

The room was small and windowless with an old wooden table and some chairs in the center. Against one wall were some cabinets and a half-size refrigerator that looked like it hadn't been cleaned in years. An older teenage girl sat at the table, smoking a cigarette between eating bites of rice from a bowl. Veata noticed the girl wore a similar red dress to hers, which contrasted sharply against the dark blue colors swirling around her.

She's sad. Very, very sad.

"She needs to be marked," Teng said to the girl.
"I've got to go back to the stage. She has a customer
waiting in stall fifteen. Take her there after you're done.
And *Rithisak* wants it done quickly."

The girl extinguished her cigarette and nodded.
After Teng left, the girl stood and pulled
something out of a cupboard.

"Come sit," she said in a flat tone. "My name is
Chemsi. What's yours?"

"Veata."

"Are you scared, Veata?"

Veata nodded.

"Good. This is a scary place. It will always be a
scary place, but the first week is the hardest. I'll help you
when I can—to make things easier. But whatever you do,
don't make Rithisak mad. Trust me, you don't want that."

Veata nodded, already scared of the large man.

"Good. Sit down and lay your arm across the
table."

Chemsi took Veata's right arm, turned it over so
the inside of her wrist was exposed, then poured a few
drops of clear liquid on her wrist and rubbed it around.

"Cheap vodka," Chemsi said. "Sterilizes the skin
and needle. They used to mark the girls without cleaning
first, but I try to keep it clean. We don't want to share
any…sickness."

Veata flinched when Chemsi flipped on a small
device with a metal pointy end and brought it toward her
wrist.

"This will hurt, like ants biting," she said evenly. "But, I will be quick. If you can be strong and not cry, I will give you a special piece of candy. I know where Teng hides the candy."

Chemsi held her arm tight, pinning it to the table, and softly sang a lullaby. Veata was surprised when she recognized the song. It was a lullaby her mother had sung to her before she died.

> *Sleep, my darling, sleep.*
> *Don't cry, my baby.*
> *Your rice with honey,*
> *Is already prepared.*

Veata's pulse quickened. The blood in her veins burned like hot coals as the vibrating needle inched closer to her wrist.

> *When you wake up*
> *I'll feed you.*
> *After you've eaten*
> *You'll play over here.*
> *If there's a chore,*
> *I'll call you,*
> *No need to go far*
> *To get you.*

The needle touched her arm, stinging like a wasp. Veata wanted to scream—to cry and pull back her wrist—but she bit her tongue, breathing hard and fast.

Don't cry, my love,
I'll hold you in my arms.
When you grow up
You'll go to school,

Chemsi choked on the word, *school,* lifting the needle for a moment. Veata watched her colors change to gray. But Chemsi quickly recovered and continued her song. Veata squeezed her eyes shut as the tattoo needle bit into her skin once again.

You'll gather knowledge,
You'll learn.
One day, my love,
It will help you.

Don't cry, my love,
I'll worry.
I need to earn a living
To take care of you.

The singing stopped.
The hum of the tattoo needle went silent.
"All done," Chemsi whispered.
Veata opened her eyes, tears falling down her cheeks. Her wrist throbbed with pain, but she was thankful the stabbing was done. She inspected the tiny black letters imprinted on her skin. There was a black

circle around them, no larger than a small coin, and a red welt swelled behind the tattoo.

"What does it say?" Veata asked through gritted teeth, trying to fight against the pain. "I can't read."

Chemsi nodded, as if expecting this. "It says, 'Sen Zi. You are now property of the Sen Zi—like me."

Chemsi held up her wrist, revealing an identical tattoo. She used a small rag to dab more of the vodka onto the new tattoo, causing Veata to flinch.

"It stings! It stings!" Veata cried.

Chemsi ignored the cries and pulled out a piece of hard candy wrapped in yellow cellophane. She twisted open the wrapper, unveiling a dark purple hard candy, and offered it to Veata.

Veata hesitated for a moment, but her stomach growled for something to eat. It was late afternoon and she'd not eaten a thing since breakfast. Snatching up the candy, she popped it into her mouth. Immediately, she welcomed the sweet fruity flavor. It tasted like a mangosteen, her favorite fruit. She savored the taste and desperately tried to hold onto the only good thing to happen to her that day—the only gift she had received on her birthday.

"It's time to go meet your first customer. I'm sorry. I can't protect you, but the candy I gave you is special—like magic. It will help dull your pain. It will help you forget."

- 4 -
Desert Eagle

A raging river of filthy water slammed James into the wall. To his side, the burly doorman hit his head against a wooden support beam and slumped on impact. James grabbed him by the collar and struggled to keep both of their heads above the rising flood.

"Munny!" James shouted, looking for his translator, though fearing the worst.

"Over here!" Munny shouted back from a dark corner of the entry room. "I right here. You okay?"

James sputtered as water rose to his neck and splashed into his face.

"No! I can't...move. Water has me...pinned. Got to...get...the inside door open," he yelled between waves of water.

James jumped up and down on his tippy-toes, still struggling to keep the guard's head above the water as well. In a few more seconds, he knew he would have to let the man go if he wanted a chance to save himself.

To his surprise, Munny nimbly climbed up a support beam, then pulled himself on top of a ceiling rafter above the inner door. With the grace of a gymnast, he swung back and forth from the rafter, gave a loud grunt, and kicked the internal door open.

Whooooosh!

A wave of water sucked James and the guard through the door, spilling them into a large, dimly lit room that looked like a nightclub. Screams echoed around them as the club filled with water—first one foot, then two feet. James propped the bouncer on the bar countertop and felt a sharp stab of pain in his bad knee.

"Munny!" he called, hoping the little gymnast was okay.

Dropping from the rafter, Munny waded inside. "I right here. You okay, Mr. Moore?"

"Sure. Couldn't be better. Thanks for asking," James said sarcastically, giving two enthusiastic thumbs up and a grim smile.

Dirty water continued to rise, now swirling past his thigh.

Scanning their surroundings, James saw a small stage with open curtains and a large glass window. A dozen or so tables and chairs were upturned, floating in the rising water, and men threw each other out of the way as they raced up a small flight of stairs in the back of the club. A handful of young girls in short red dresses screamed as they struggled to move in the same direction, being pushed back behind the men as they fled.

James had never been one to follow the crowd, but in this instance, it seemed appropriate.

"Help me with this clown," he shouted to Munny, heaving the bouncer's arm over his shoulder. The sharp pain in his knee intensified under the weight of the extra man, and the water was now lapping at his waist.

Munny hurried over to help, throwing the bouncer's other arm over his shoulder at an odd angle since he was so much shorter than James. Together they dragged the man across the room and up a handful of steps that led to a narrow hallway. The steps took them high enough to get out of the dirty water, but James feared it would not last long as the flood waters crept up the stairs behind them.

The dim hall lights flickered for a few seconds before the power went out. James pulled out his cell phone, amazed it still worked after being submerged in the water, and used it as a flashlight.

"We need to be careful," Munny whispered as they followed the crowd down the hallway. "This is bad place with bad men."

James nodded. "I kind of guessed that after this moron waved a gun in my face."

"It not just gun. Tattoo on his arm," Munny said, pointing to a circular tattoo on the man's inner-forearm. It had a Cambodian symbol that looked like the letter T with three stars surrounding it. "He part of Sen Zi. They is mafia. Bad karma. Very bad karma."

After seeing the stage and the young girls, James had his own suspicions what a mafia like the Sen Zi used this place for. They turned a corner in the hallway, entering a long room, and his suspicions were confirmed.

Dim, hazy light filtered through a few small windows covered in newspaper. The flood water had reached their ankles and was still rising.

The retreating mass of men and girls ran toward another flight in the middle of the room. Against the walls to their left and right, James made out rows of restroom-like stalls with brown curtains across them. From inside the stalls, men flung open the curtains as they heard the tumult outside and struggled to dress themselves amid the shock of rising water.

In each stall was a small, dirty cot. On each cot there was a young girl. Some of the girls were half-naked while others still wore red dresses.

James' stomach curled at the sight and bile rose up his throat.

This is sick. These girls are no older than my granddaughters.

The thought sent a wave of boiling heat through his old bones. The pain in his knee was forgotten, replaced with mounting anger.

Above the fierce clamor of those fighting to escape up the stairs, James thought he heard a scream for help. The words were in Khmer, but he didn't need a translator to know what they meant.

"Help! Please help!"

"Do you hear that?" James asked Munny, spinning in a circle as he tried to pinpoint the sound. "Someone's calling for help."

Munny shook his head. "I hear nothing, beside people screaming who go up stairs. We need go too. Water keep coming."

James nodded dismissively. "I know, I know. But listen. Can't you hear it? Those screams! Where are they coming from?"

James slid the unconscious bouncer off his shoulder and draped him over a table. Turning his head to the side, he closed his eyes and cupped his hands around his ears.

"Help! Someone help us!" faint voices cried out again. It was coming from the dark shadows of the far corner of the room. James moved closer, sloshing through the water, and saw a closed door.

"I hear it now," Munny said, following close behind James.

James struggled to pull the door open against the rising water, but with Munny's help they forced it open. High-pitched screams of terror came from inside the pitch black room. Shining his phone into the room, James jumped backward as dozens of snakes and rats swam out of the doorway. They slipped around him while some tried to climb up his body.

Both he and Munny jumped up and down in the water, shouting curses as they swatted the creatures away. But their shouts were overpowered by the shrieks coming from inside.

James fought back the fear of the snakes and rats, pushing through the doorway into the darkness. Shining his light against a wall, he gasped.

In the room was a square metal cage with six girls locked inside. The young girls yelled for help as the water continued to rise, submerging them from their ribs down. One of the girls, an older looking teenager, held a small child in her arms as she desperately swatted snakes and rats off of them that were trying to escape the water. Munny went to open the cage, but found a heavy padlock over the door.

"Take my phone!" James told Munny. "I have an idea. Tell the girls it will be alright. We will protect them."

Munny's face was pale with shock and he stood frozen, mumbling something to himself.

"Munny!" James shouted, shaking the young man by the arm. "Take—my—phone. Pull it together, man. I need you to try to calm the girls down and I'll be right back."

Munny blinked at James, seeming to come out of a trance, and nodded. He let go of his wrist and took the phone, a new look of determination crossing his face, and he started speaking to the girls.

James rushed from the room of horrors, thankful to find the bouncer still slumped over the table. Rolling him over, he yanked the handgun from his back waistband and read the words, *.50 Caliber Desert Eagle,* engraved along the barrel.

"I hope this does the trick," he muttered, hefting the large pistol.

James remembered watching a TV show where they shot high powered guns into a pool of water to see if the myth of diving under water could save you from being shot like it does in the movies. Surprisingly, it had worked, causing most of the bullets shot from high-powered rifles to break apart on impact with the water. He hoped the water would offer some protection to the girls from possible ricochets.

But none of that matters if I can't get the lock off.

Wading back into the room, Munny shone the light on James, nearly blinding him.

"Shine that on the lock," he yelled at Munny, shielding his eyes from the bright light until Munny pointed it at the cage.

"Good. Now tell the girls to scoot back and duck under the water on the count of three!"

Munny nodded and spoke to the girls.

"Okay. One!"

Munny repeated the count in Khmer.

"Two!"

James took aim at the lock.

"Three!"

Making sure the girls were underwater, he fired.

- 5 -
Property

Veata's stomach churned and her tongue felt numb after swallowing the last of the candy. She held Chemsi's hand as the older girl led her upstairs to the next floor and down a hallway to another room. A young man sat in front of the entrance, which was lined with hanging brown beads instead of a door, and stared intently at a game he was playing on his phone. He looked up, gave them a cursory glance, and went back to playing his game. Veata watched his colors fade back and forth between dark brown and tan as he moved the phone side-to-side like it was a steering wheel.

"New girl?" he asked, keeping his eyes focused on his phone.

"Yes," Chemsi replied.

"Take her to bed fifteen. Customer is waiting."

Chemsi sneered at the man as she walked past and gave Veata's hand a gentle squeeze once they pushed past the beads.

The room was long, spanning most of the second floor of the building. Fluorescent lights were strung across the ceiling and a few small windows were covered in newspaper, letting in a small amount of natural light.

But the light wasn't enough to brighten the dingy room, and Veata covered her nose against the strong musty smell mixed with incense. Lining one wall were rows of stalls with curtains covering them.

Veata heard strange noises coming from the stalls and gripped Chemsi's hand tighter.

Chemsi pulled her along until they came in front of a stall near the end of the room. Veata's stomach twisted like she had swallowed knives, and sweat beaded up along her forehead.

"I don't feel good," she mumbled to Chemsi, holding her stomach. "It's so hot...and my stomach hurts."

"You have to go in now. It will be over fast—like the tattoo. I don't have any customers right now. I'll wait outside to help you after."

The curtain slid open, revealing the man with the mustache who had called Veata's number when she was on stage. His shirt was off, and his colors sparked violet and red.

"Finally," he hissed. "What took so long? I've been waiting."

"My apologies," Chemsi said with a sharp tone. "She had to meet with the owner, *Rithisak,* first."

The man seemed to calm down at the mention of Rithisak's name, the red in his color disappearing, turning a shade of yellow. But when he looked down at Veata, his colors flared violet again.

Chemsi gently tried to push Veata into the tiny stall, but Veata shook her head, digging her heels into floor. But the man was tired of waiting. He grabbed Veata under the arms and lifted her small frame off the ground, carrying her into the stall with one arm while closing the curtain with the other.

Veata groaned as he tossed her onto a cot covered with a stained sheet. Her stomach felt like someone was stabbing her and she clenched her jaw in pain.

The man bent over her, his face so close she felt his hot, smelly breath against her neck. She fought to push him away, pressing her hands against his face when he tried to kiss her.

"None of that," he growled, grabbing both of her hands and holding them tightly above her head.

Veata cried out, desperately trying to wriggle free, but the man would not let go. He leaned in to kiss her again and she kicked. She kicked as hard as she could in the place she knew it hurt boys the most.

The man's grip on her arms slipped free and he groaned. She kicked again in the same place and the man backed away a step, doubling over in agony. With his head in striking distance, she kicked again and again, connecting with his face twice more before the exertion proved too much.

The room began to spin in a circle and her stomach burned as if it was on fire. The fire crept up her chest, into her throat, and exploded from her mouth in a barrage of vomit that covered the shirtless man.

He yelled in disgust, swiping vomit from his face and chest, when Veata threw up again, this time all over his legs and feet.

A cold shiver ran through her veins, and she started to shake.

"So cold," she mumbled, trying to stop herself from shaking, but her body would not relent.

The customer screamed with rage, trying to shake the vomit from his bare chest and pants. The stall curtain whipped open and the man who had been playing games on his phone looked at the scene, reeling back as he wrinkled his nose in disgust.

Veata heard the customer yell about being kicked, the vomit, and something about demanding a refund. But Veata didn't care. She just curled up in a ball on the cot, whimpering as she shivered.

Chemsi pushed past the men and lifted Veata into her arms.

"Chemsi," Veata moaned, her teeth chattering uncontrollably. "I don't...feel...good."

"I know. I'm here," Chemsi whispered into her ear, holding Veata close. She carried her out of the room with the stalls and away from the yelling customer and his insults.

"I'm sorry, Veata," Chemsi said, holding Veata tightly as she convulsed in her arms. "It's my fault. I shouldn't have given you the candy. You're too young for it. It made you sick."

"You...you made me...sick?" Veata asked, her teeth rattling.

Chemsi nodded. "Not on purpose. I'm sorry. I just didn't want you to feel it and be hurt. I was trying to help. I am—"

But Chemsi went silent and Veata felt the girl's body stiffen. Looking up, she saw Teng barreling down the hallway toward them, his colors blood-red and sour.

"Stupid girl!" Teng hissed at Veata. "You cost us money!"

"But she's sick," Chemsi retorted. "She didn't know any better."

"Do you think Rithisak cares? We had to promise the guy free drinks and two free girls on his next visit. She needs to learn a lesson. Take her to the cage."

Chemsi shook her head. "No."

Teng raised an eyebrow. "What did you say?"

"No! She's sick. She has a fever. Let her sleep it off in an empty cot."

Teng's hand shot out with a vicious slap across Chemsi's face. Despite the blow, Chemsi stood firm and Veata curled her head into the older girl's chest.

Teng let loose a string of swears and gripped Chemsi by the arm, dragging them both into a nearby room. Inside, four other girls were resting on a dirty couch, waiting for their next customers. Dark circles hung under their eyes, which looked glossed over, and a pile of empty candy wrappers were tossed on the floor.

"But it's only her first day, Teng," Chemsi pleaded as he closed the door behind them. "Don't send her to the cage. She's sick. She could die if you leave her in there."

The other girls seemed to wake from their fog at the sight of Chemsi, Veata, and Teng.

"She a new girl?" one asked. "Been awhile since we had a new one."

"So little," another said.

"Teng wants to send her to the cage," Chemsi told the girls. "But she's sick. It's her first day."

Three of the girls on the couch shook their heads, murmuring their disapproval, while one looked annoyed by the commotion.

"C'mon, Teng. Let her be," said one girl.

"She's no good sick," chimed another.

The annoyed girl flipped her long black hair behind her ear and rolled her eyes. "Whatever," she breathed. "Send her to the cage. Who cares? She's got to learn some time."

Chemsi and the other girls shot her a menacing glare. "Shut up, Shukira!" Chemsi spat. "No one asked you."

Shukira raised an eyebrow and shook her head dismissively before popping another candy into her mouth. "You can't protect her forever, *Chemsi*."

Ignoring Shukira, another girl with wide-set eyes slipped next to Teng and reached her hand up behind his neck, curling his black hair in her fingers. "Won't you give her a break, Teng—for me. She's new and we'll show her how it works tomorrow."

Indecision flitted across Teng's face and he slowly shook his head. "I don't know girls. Rithisak is going to be furious. She needs to learn a lesson."

"I know," said the girl with her fingers still in his hair. Her other hand crawled up his chest and she gave him a pouty lip. "We'll teach her tomorrow. But for now, let her sleep. I'll make it up to you."

Teng raised an eyebrow and smiled. "*Well,* maybe we'll let it pass this one time. But I really shouldn't."

"You're right. You shouldn't!" a voice barked from behind them.

Veata saw a violent storm of deep black and dark red swirl into the room. It was Rithisak.

He grabbed Teng by the hair and slammed his head into a nearby wall. Teng fell back a step, dazed, but Rithisak didn't stop. The large man punched him in the stomach and then once more in the face.

"I warned you—no more mistakes! I know you've been sneaking off with the girls during work hours. I know you've been stealing bottles of vodka from the bar. Not only will I teach you a lesson, but I'll personally beat your mother and brother before I kick them out into the street from the room I so graciously let you rent from the Sen Zi."

Rithisak slammed his fist across Teng's face one more time before Teng collapsed to the ground. He turned to the girls, a low growl resonating deep in his throat.

"You are *all* property of the Sen Zi. You work for *me!* And if you're not working, you're not making money. And if you're not making money, you must be taught to improve your work ethic."

Three other men came into the room, each holding a wooden baton in their hands.

"Take them all to the cage," Rithisak commanded. "No food. No water. No candy for three days."

- 6 -

Up On the Rooftop

James felt his ears explode as he fired two deafening shots at the lock on the cage.

Munny, who'd been shining a light on the lock from a distance, waded closer for a better look and whooped with excitement.

"Lock broken!" he shouted before pumping his fist in the air.

James released a long sigh, only then realizing he'd been holding his breath. He pushed the safety on the gun and tucked it into his back waistband, which was now under the rising water. The girls waded out of their dark prison, some of them practically swimming as they hurried to escape along with the rats and snakes.

An older teen was still pressed against the cage, struggling to hold a small child above the water. James reached out, offering to hold the child, but the older teen retracted.

"It's okay," James said softly. "Munny, tell her it's okay before they both drown."

After Munny translated, the teen hesitated a moment, but finally relented and handed the small girl into his outstretched arms.

"Thank you," James said. "I know I'm a big, ugly, scary looking old guy, and you have no idea what I'm saying, but I'm here to help."

The group sloshed through the water into the main room and headed to the staircase where the others had fled to seek higher ground.

"Hey, where's the guard?" James asked as they passed a floating table. It was the same table he'd left the unconscious thug lying on only a few minutes earlier.

Munny shrugged. "Who cares? He drown, or wake and go up the stairs. *We* need go now or we drown too!"

James nodded. There wasn't time to search for him. Their priority was getting these girls to safety. He led the group up the stairs with Munny at the rear.

James breathed hard as he struggled up the dark stairwell, his body rebelling against the unplanned exercise. Midway up, a sharp pain stabbed into his knee and caused the joint to buckle under him. He nearly dropped the girl, moaning in pain as he gripped the handrail to steady himself. A hot flame spread from his knee, up his hamstring and down the side of his calf, forcing him to lean against the wall for relief.

"You okay?" Munny asked from behind as the group came to a halt.

"Fine," James growled. "I'm fine. Just need a quick break." Still holding the child in one arm, he pressed his eyes closed and tried to push back the pain while taking deep breaths. His knee felt like it was swollen larger than a watermelon and he could barely bend it anymore.

"You injured?" Munny called. "I come help you."

"No! Just give me a second," James called back, knowing he was too big for Munny to help. "There's a balcony door up ahead. We're almost there."

James repositioned the shivering girl to his other arm. He gritted his teeth and took a step, then another, and another. The rickety stairs creaked and groaned, and he worried the whole thing would collapse under his weight, but it held together as he limped along. He looked up the next flight of stairs to the balcony door. It was slightly ajar and a glimmer of daylight shone through the opening. The light seemed to beckon him forward, giving him something else to focus on beside the searing pain in his leg.

James had never been so thankful for light as when he pulled the door open and stepped out into the fresh air. Rain drizzled from billowing pale gray clouds, and even though he was already soaked from the flood, it felt as if the rain and the light were washing him clean from the hellish scene below.

From the third story balcony, he peeked over the railing to find a debris-filled river flowing through the street. To his left, a short metal ladder continued up the side of the building to the rooftop where James figured everyone else had gone.

The little girl in his arms felt light as a feather as she clung to him like a koala bear. But seeing her in the light of day increased his worry. Her lips were purple and she was shivering uncontrollably in her wet, red dress.

He pulled her closer, resting her head on his shoulder like he'd done hundreds of times with his own daughters when they had been little. He carefully climbed the ladder, thankful it was only a few feet high. When he pulled himself over the last rung he found a small crowd of men and girls gathered on the far side of the flat rooftop.

He climbed onto the roof and helped the next girl climb up. It was the older teen who'd been holding the child before. She held her hands out to take the little girl back from James' arms. This time it was James who hesitated to release her, but he relented under the teen's hard stare.

After handing off the child, he turned to help the next girl onto the roof when he heard a scream from behind. He turned to find two men dragging away the teen with the little girl in her arms. To his surprise, one of them was the bald bouncer he'd saved from drowning.

They seemed to ignore James, shouting at the teen as they pulled her by the hair and dragged her toward a group of other girls in red dresses who'd been corralled in a corner of the roof.

Blood burned through his veins, rushing up to his head until dots of light flashed in his vision. The pain in his knee was forgotten and his exhaustion disappeared, replaced with uncontrollable fury.

"Let them go!" he snapped, charging like a raging bull.

Reaching the men in a few long steps, he grabbed them both by their throats, one in each hand, and squeezed with a vice-like grip until they let go of the teenage girl.

With a strength he had not felt since being an offensive lineman in college over forty years ago, he pulled them toward his towering figure and shoved them away with a guttural yell.

The two men fell over one another, holding their throats as they coughed and sputtered. The bald bouncer found his legs and stood up, yelling at James in Khmer and pointing his finger at him and at the girls.

"Everything okay, Mr. Moore?" Munny called from the balcony below. "I hear shouting."

"Hurry up!" James yelled over his shoulder, keeping his eyes on the two men. "Things are about to get ugly."

A plump man with a greasy black ponytail and a red Hawaiian looking shirt approached the scene and the two thugs parted ways for him.

The man was large, more fat than muscle, but he was not as big as James and stood about a head shorter. He stuck his chin out proudly as he came face-to-face with James, and gave a head nod while pointing to the girls behind him.

James stared him down and shook his head.

The fat man's face burned red and he broke into a tirade of yelling, waving his arms like a wild man while pointing back and forth at James and the girls coming up the ladder.

The fat man took a step closer, spittle spewing from his mouth. James felt it spray on his face and he clenched his fists, about to punch the guy square in chin, when Munny hopped on the roof and dashed to his side.

The man continued to shout and Munny quickly translated. "He says the girls have to come with him. He is their owner and the girls are his."

James shook his head, his chest heaving back and forth as he fought to control his anger. "I'll never let those girls go back with him. Tell *tubby* he has two options. Option A, leave the girls alone, I report them to the police, and they get arrested. Option B is similar to option A, but involves me beating the snot out of him before I toss his worthless hide off the building and into the flood."

Munny raised an eyebrow. "You sure that wise thing to say?"

James nodded, still glaring at the men. He knew it was three against two, but he was a big guy and had been in his fair share of scuffles growing up. And even though he was old, at this moment he felt like he could take on the world. Part of him hoped they chose Option B.

"Just repeat my words exactly," James assured Munny. "Those are their options."

Munny shook his head in mild disbelief and spoke to the men. But to James' surprise, the three thugs started laughing. The fat man held his belly, nearly doubling over as he chuckled.

"What is it?" James asked, their laughter fueling his anger. "What, they don't think I'm serious?"

Munny shrugged.

A girl stepped up behind Munny and whispered into his ear.

"Um, James. We small problem have with your options. The bald man you save downstairs, he local police. He work as bouncer on weekend and is customer too. Lots of police are customers. Police not help us here."

The fat owner's laughter came to an end and he let out a whistle, raising his hand to call over an additional two thugs to his side. The owner stepped forward and spoke, frothing from the mouth like a rabid dog.

"He wants to know your name," Munny said. "But I would not tell—"

"James Moore," James replied, cutting Munny off. "My name is James Moore."

The owner snorted. "James Moore. You dead man." he said in a heavy accent. As he did this, James noticed a tattoo of a snake inked across the knuckles of the owner's right hand.

A childhood memory flashed through his mind. He was ten years-old, visiting his grandfather's ranch in west Texas. A poisonous copperhead had slithered into the stables and caught him off guard as he fed grains to a young colt. But before the snake could strike, his grandfather came out of nowhere, swinging a shovel, and whacked the head clean off the snake. "You want to kill a snake," his grandfather had said, sounding just like John Wayne, "you gotta to take off its head."

I just got to take down the leader, James thought. *But now it's five on two. I really hope Munny knows how to fight.*

As if reading James mind, Munny spoke. "I hope you know how to fight. I take three on left. You take fat owner and bald policeman on right. I help as soon as I finish three men."

"Wait, what?" James asked, cocking his head as he looked at Munny's diminutive frame.

Munny was still holding James' phone and held up one hand toward the brothel thugs, as if asking for a timeout, and then passed the phone back to Chemsi. "Okay, now I ready. Did not want to break your phone. It nice iPhone," Munny said with a wide grin. "We punch on three. Okay. One, two," but before Munny reached three he unleashed a lightning speed roundhouse kick to the neck of one of the thugs on the left.

"Three!" Munny shouted.

- 7 -
Don't Shoot

Veata welcomed the warm rays of sunshine as they punched holes through the thinning gray clouds above. The stabbing pains in her stomach were finally gone, but she still felt weak and cold.

Chemsi held her close, but part of her wished the old giant was still holding her. He was much warmer than Chemsi and his big arms had wrapped around her like a blanket.

"They're going to get themselves killed," Veata heard Chemsi mutter. "They can't fight Rithisak. He has too many men."

Veata watched as her giant traded vicious blows with Rithisak. Surges of the giant's silver light clashed against the black storm that surrounded the brothel owner. After punching Rithisak in the stomach, the giant grabbed him by the ponytail and pulled his head downward into a hard uppercut to the face.

CRACK!

Veata flinched at the sound of bone crunching against bone. A second attacker, a bald man in a tank top, ran at the giant from behind.

"Behind you!" Veata tried to yell, but her throat was sore and her voice came out weak and raspy. In that moment, she also forgot that he spoke a different language.

Unable to hear, or understand her, the giant was unprepared when the second attacker snuck up behind and kicked him square in the back.

The giant fell like a towering tree in the jungle. He tried to push himself onto his hands and knees, but the bald attacker kicked him in the ribs once, twice, and a third time, sending the giant rolling onto his back. Veata saw one eye starting to swell and streams of crimson blood ran down his face from his nose and a cut on his cheekbone.

A few feet to the side, the old giant's friend, Munny she thought she'd heard Chemsi call him, was fighting like a mongoose surrounded by cobras. Veata had once seen a mongoose take on a Thai Spitting Cobra in her village. Moving fast as lightning, the mongoose struck the back of the cobra's hood and wrestled it to the ground before killing it.

Munny seemed to move even faster than a mongoose as he avoided the attacks of three men. He twisted, jumped, and rolled while delivering fast strikes that sent all three men to the ground over and over again.

"Munny is doing amazing," Chemsi said, a hint of admiration in her voice, "but the big guy, James, is in trouble."

"We'll be in bigger trouble when Rithisak is done with them," one of the girls standing next to them said. "He might kill us too...or worse."

"What should we do, Chemsi?" another girl asked.

Chemsi did not respond, her eyes transfixed on the fight.

"I can't go back," a fourth girl whimpered. "I've tried to escape before. I know what Rithisak will do when he gets us. I'll jump in the water and drown before he takes me again."

"No," Chemsi scolded the girl. "You will stay with us, Somaly. We stick together."

"Where would we even go if we did escape?" an older girl spat. "You're all idiots. I'm sneaking over with the rest of the girls. I had nothing to do with any of this!"

Chemsi grabbed the girl by the shoulder and shoved her away from them. "Go ahead, Shukira. You can be Rithisak's play toy and rat. I know you were the one who turned in Somaly when she tried to get away. You're worse than Rithisak, you chn kabat."

Chn kabat, Veata thought. *Traitor.* Her uncle had once called her a traitor, after he'd forced her to help him cheat at a card game. Even with her help, he'd still lost. She'd received a beating for it.

Shukira shot Chemsi a dark scowl, slinking away to where the other girls and customers were gathered.

Veata looked at the other group of girls. There were at least twenty of them, all young teenagers wearing red dresses and lots of makeup. To their side were a few dozen customers watching the fight with equal interest, but they did not join the fight. They only watched.

The giant named James fought his way back to his feet. Wrapping his thick arms around the second attacker, he lifted him upside down and drove the man head first into the hard roof.

CRACK!

The bald man's ash brown colors stopped spinning. They faded until a low glow settled around his motionless body.

Veata had seen the colors depart from others before, like her mother and father when they died. But this man's colors remained. They were weak, but he was not dead.

Rithisak's face a mess of swelling bruises, and blood ran from his nose like a faucet as he shuffled toward James.

James' chest heaved in and out with heavy breaths, like a man who had just sprinted in a race.

Rithisak bent down, lifted his pant leg, and pulled a long knife from inside his boot. "I kill you," he spat, blood spraying from his lips. Veata shivered when his stormy colors turned into a pitch-black abyss, seeming to snuff out any nearby light.

He pointed the knife at Veata and the girls around her. "Then," he snarled, "I kill girls."

James' eyes widened at the sight of the knife, but when Rithisak threatened the girls, Veata had to shield her eyes from the sudden flare in James' brightness. Rays of silver light wrapped around the giant like gleaming armor, pushing back the overwhelming darkness around Rithisak.

As the light grew brighter, a smile stretched across James' face and he casually reached back behind him to pull a gun from his waistband. Pointing the weapon into the air, he fired three times.

BANG! BANG! BANG!

Everyone froze.

Rithisak's black storm faded into a pale shade of yellow and he dropped his knife to the ground.

James pointed the gun at Rithisak and for a brief moment Veata saw a flash of darkness replace the silver light around James. It went back to silver, then to black, then silver again.

Veata's body suddenly stopped shaking and she felt renewed strength course through her veins. She wiggled free from Chemsi's arms, but Chemsi quickly pulled her back.

"Stop! What are you doing? Are you trying to get yourself killed?" Chemsi asked.

"I have to help him," Veata pleaded, fighting to shake free from Chemsi's grasp.

"No, you don't," Chemsi replied, struggling to hold Veata in place. "It's too dangerous."

Chemsi's grip tightened and Veata did the first thing that came to mind, she sank her teeth into Chemsi's arm.

Chemsi yelped, loosening her grip just enough for Veata to wiggle free and dash toward James.

She watched James stare at her in disbelief as she ran toward him, his head bouncing back and forth between her and Rithisak while the gun stayed trained on the brothel owner.

Veata slowed to a stop in front of James and rested her small hand on the forearm of his outstretched hand with the gun.

His eyes narrowed and looked down on her from high above, shaking his head in confusion.

"Kom Banh," Veata pleaded in Khmer. "Don't shoot."

- 8 -
Bright Colors

This gun is so heavy. Why is it so heavy? James thought.

He couldn't believe he'd forgotten about the large pistol stashed in his back waistband. But when the fight had broken out, his mind was filled with such utter rage that he'd completely forgotten about the gun, especially since a firearm was not something he carried in normal life.

Footsteps charged at him from the left and he twisted, pointing the weapon at the source. He blinked rapidly, hesitating as a surprised Munny skidded to a halt upon having a gun aimed at his face.

"No shoot! No shoot!" Munny yelped.

"Idiot!" James hissed. "I could have killed you!"

"I sorry," Munny replied, shaking his hands out in front of his chest as if they were shields. "You move gun now, please. No kill Munny."

James realized he still had the gun aimed at Munny's head and took a dazed step back, looking at the foreign object in his hand. Out of the corner of his eye, he saw the brothel owner move toward him and he whipped the gun back around, training it on the man.

The brothel owner froze, glaring at James through his bloodied face.

Adrenaline pumped through James' veins and his eyes darted back and forth between the brothel owner, his men—most of which Munny had left writhing in pain on the ground—and Munny himself.

Then he saw the girls huddled together, shivering and cold in their skimpy red dresses. Heat ran up his spine like a raging fire and he felt the anger explode anew in his mind. He slipped his finger onto the trigger and aimed straight at the brothel owner's chest.

You're dead. I'm going to end you, you evil son of a—

But his thoughts were interrupted by a movement to his side. A little girl in a red dress—the same girl he had carried out of the flood—walked directly toward him. Small as she was, wearing nothing more than a tattered dress, she looked almost regal as she calmly walked across the rooftop amidst the stunned stares of onlookers.

With her head high and her hands at her side, her brown eyes locked with James' as she approached.

He saw a light there. A peaceful, bright light in her eyes. It seemed to expand across her whole body in a yellow glow that shone like the sun at noonday.

The child reached him and rested her tiny hand on his outstretched forearm. He felt the gun tremble in his hand.

So heavy. So blasted heavy.

"Kom banh," the girl said softly.

James shook his head, confused. "What?" he whispered.

The little girl spoke again, repeating the same phrase, "kom banh."

"What did she say?" James asked Munny.

"She say, 'don't shoot,'" Munny translated.

James looked down at the child in disbelief. He shook his head. He wanted to shoot the brothel owner. It was no longer about self defense or saving the girls. He wanted to kill the man.

The girl gently squeezed his forearm. He watched in amazement as the golden light from her hand swirled around his arm and flowed up his shoulder.

"What are you doing? What is this light? What are you doing to me?"

Munny gave James a concerned look. "What light, James? I see nothing."

James turned to Munny. "What do you mean, what light? Don't you see it? It's coming from her. It's going up my arm. It's so bright. Almost blinding."

Munny shook his head.

Am I the only one seeing this? Am I going crazy? James thought.

The child's large brown eyes pierced him to the core as the golden swirls wrapped up his neck and around his head. It seemed to cool his rage, but he resisted, his emotions going back and forth between hatred and hope.

"But if I shoot him," he sputtered to the girl. "I can end this now. You can all be free! Tell her Munny. Tell her what I said."

Munny looked uneasy as he translated James' words. When he finished, the girl only shook her head.

"But why?" James screamed. "Why shouldn't I kill him? He deserves to die!"

This time when Munny translated, the girl spoke slow and soft.

"Your colors. Don't let the darkness kill your bright colors."

When Munny translated her words, James felt like he'd been punched in the gut. For years he'd felt a misty darkness hovering over him like a black rain cloud that he could never escape. He recognized the darkness—the anger and the hatred—and he knew it was trying to overpower him.

His quick temper and blistering anger had cost him his first marriage. His newfound wealth and long periods on the road had cost him his second. His selfish neglect had cost him time with his children and grandchildren, making him a stranger to them. And in this moment, he knew his next actions would come at a cost.

Your colors, he repeated in his mind. *Don't let the darkness kill your bright colors.*

Unable to fight back the tears, he felt his emotions break like a ship against a rock. "Do I have any colors left?" he whimpered, tasting the mix of salt water and blood on his lips.

The little girl nodded and then gave him the most unexpected and perfect gift he could imagine. She hugged him.

James' heart swelled. It felt like it would burst. For years he'd felt lost, like a ship without a rudder, driving away everyone he loved and cared for in the process. Life had lost its purpose—its luster—its color. But now, of all times, after everything that he'd just been through, he felt a growing measure of hope.

Maybe...maybe I can start over. Maybe I can have a second chance.

With his free hand, James returned her embrace, welcoming the unconditional love of this little child. She'd been through more than he could imagine, yet here she was comforting him.

"What's your name?" he asked the girl.

With tears in his own eyes, Munny translated and the girl responded.

"Veata. My name is Veata."

James smiled, letting the gun slowly falling to his side as he gave the girl another hug.

"Thank you, Veata."

He wiped his bloodied, tear-streamed face against his sleeve, soaking in the light of this little girl as he tried to regain his composure. But the moment was cut short when Munny shouted, "Watch out!"

- 9 -
Monster

Veata felt James' grip tighten around her arm as he pulled her back behind his hulking frame. The darkness around him had disappeared, replaced by a rainbow of bright colors. Peeking around his leg, she saw Rithisak running at him with a knife in his hand.

The world seemed to slow as James raised the gun. This time his colors did not flicker dark, but stayed bright and true.

He pulled the trigger.

CLICK. CLICK. CLICK.

Nothing happened.

There was no explosion from the weapon like before, only the quiet click of the trigger.

Rithisak reached them in two more steps, preparing to plunge his dagger into James chest.

James tried to maneuver to the side, but his knee buckled as he twisted and he fell to the ground. Veata screamed, watching the sharp, shining blade arc down at James. But just before it hit, Munny's foot kicked upward with lightning speed, striking Rithisak's arm.

Veata gasped as the blade went flying through the air only inches from her face.

Munny slammed his other foot into the side of Rithisak's head, sending the brothel owner sprawling across the rooftop.

Veata held James' hand as he struggled to stand back up and Munny took a defensive position in front of them.

Now that the gun was out of ammunition, Rithisak's men rallied with newfound courage. Though beaten and bruised, they helped Rithisak to his feet and sneered at James and Munny as their own colors flashed between black and red.

James grimaced and pulled himself to his feet, favoring his good leg as he stood. Blood trickled down his swollen cheek and he said something to Munny, but Veata did not understand his language. Munny replied to James in English before letting off a string of swear words in Khmer.

I know those words, Veata thought. *Uncle only said those when things were really bad after a night of gambling.*

She watched Rithisak and his men prowl forward like a pack of wild, injured dogs, and she knew things *were* really, really bad this time.

"I can't fight them all myself," Munny said to no one as he and James took a step back.

"You don't have to," a familiar voice called as she stepped next to Munny.

It was Chemsi.

"I won't let him torture me anymore," she said. "I won't!"

Another girl, Somaly, stepped forward to join Chemsi. "He killed my sister and you all know what he did to me when I tried to run away," she said to the other girls. "I'll die fighting before I let him touch me again."

A handful of girls started nodding and stepped forward to join them.

"But we have nowhere else to go!" Shukira shouted, tears forming in her eyes. "I have no one else. I have no family. I have no one and no place except here."

Veata watched Shukira's colors flicker between dark blue and charcoal.

"She's scared," Veata whispered. "So very scared."

"We have each other!" Chemsi shouted back. "We stick together or we die."

Most of the girls nodded, but a few hung back together by Shukira, unwilling to move.

"He'll kill me after this! You all know he will," Chemsi said to the remaining girls huddled by Shukira. "But it doesn't matter. Eventually, he will kill us all! Remember Chantrea? He didn't let her go when she got too old looking. He shot her. And when Jarani got pregnant, he had a doctor give her an abortion, but she died three days later with an infection."

Veata saw the colors in the girls, which had been dull and a faded gray, flicker to life as Chemsi spoke. Soon bright sparks ignited in girl after girl, including Shukira and her group.

"And you all remember what he did to Kun Thea," Chemsi continued, her voice low and mournful. "She was just a girl, younger than Veata." Chemsi pulled Veata into a side hug and held her tight. The colorful lights of all the girls grew brighter like a flame spreading into a wildfire. "She was your friend, Shukira. And when Kun Thea got sick with the AIDS, he...he…"

Chemsi eyed Shukira, but couldn't finish, choking on her words.

The dark fear in Shukira's colors disappeared into a pulsing red and purple. She looked at Rithisak, her lips trembling, and hissed. "Besach."

"Besach," another girl repeated. "He's a monster."

"Besach," Shukira said louder. "Monster. Monster. Monster."

The other girls took up the chant, "Besach. Besach. Besach."

Soon all of the girls' colors were stoked in bright wonder. Even Shukira started to chant, her dark colors shining bright. Slowly they stepped forward, spreading out around Rithisak and his men.

The air buzzed with electricity as the girls continued to chant, "Besach. Besach. Besach." The sight gave Veata goosebumps as she watched the girls close in around the men—no longer the hunted, but the hunters.

The customers seemed to sense it too, backing away even further from the girls until they were pushed against the far side of the rooftop with their backs to the edge.

"Besach! Besach! Besach!" the girls yelled louder, only a few feet away from the men.

"Shut up!" Rithisak screamed, his face a disfigured mess from the beating James had given him. He swore at them, cursed them, and called them every bad word Veata knew and a few she had never heard before.

The girls ignored him, moving closer, and closer, and closer.

"Besach! Besach! Besach!"

Rithisak's men gathered together, and Veata saw the fear in their colors as thirty girls closed around them like a noose.

"I'll kill you all!" Rithisak shouted. "I can always get more girls. You're worthless. Used. I don't need you!"

The buzzing grew louder in Veata's ears and seemed ready to burst. Rithisak grabbed the closest girl by the hair, yanked the poor girl to the ground, and was about to kick her in the face when they swarmed.

Twenty-nine girls, in Twenty-nine red dresses, attacked like an angry nest of hornets.

Veata stayed behind James watching the scene unfold. Munny and James took a few steps forward, trying to help in the fight, but Rithisak and his men were nearly invisible behind the fray of red surrounding them. The girls kicked, bit, scratched, punched, and stomped on the men. They yelled curses and screamed at the top of their lungs, letting all their pent-up anger and pain pour from their souls.

The men tried to fight back, striking a few girls with their blows. But the punishment was not new to them. They'd been hit before. It would not stop their furious assault.

Within a few minutes, all five men lay on the ground—motionless.

Chemsi stood over Rithisak, breathing hard. "You kidnapped me. Took me from my home. Beat me. Raped me. Drugged me. Mr. James may lose his color if he kills you. But I can't find mine until you're gone."

Veata stepped toward Chemsi, but Chemsi held up her hand. "No, Veata," she said, shaking her head. "Stay back. We have to do this."

Like a military general, Chemsi gave orders to the other girls. They lifted the men one by one into the air and threw them over the side of the roof into the waters below.

Rithisak was the last to be lifted, his eyes going in and out of consciousness. A dozen girls worked together to support his bulk as they carried him to the edge. With each step, Chemsi spoke, her voice growing louder.

"This is for Chantrea!" Chemsi called out.

Step.

"This is for Jarani!"

Step.

"This is for Somaly and her sister!"

Step.

"This is for Kun Thea!"

The group stopped at the edge of the building and Chemsi whispered in Rithisak's ear. "You should have taken Mr. James' option A."

With a nod of her head, the girls hefted the brothel owner over the edge of the building. His body hit the water with a splash and Veata watched his faint colors disappear from view.

- 10 -
Drop in the Bucket

"You want to run that by me again?" James asked. "Did you say we have twenty-four kilometers to go? As in the numbers two-four?"

Munny nodded. "Yes, I say twenty-four. Is my accent hard to understand? Sometime English numbers hard for me to speak. I forget to—"

James waved his hand. "No! I understood you clearly! But Munny, twenty-four kilometers? If my math's right, that's like fifteen miles. I thought you said this place was close? Fifteen miles is not close! Close is a quick walk around the block. Close means we get there before nightfall."

"But it is close. It only just outside city."

James sighed.

"I repeat. Fifteen miles is not close, especially when you're walking through a war zone with no food, water, and a leg that's ready to snap off!"

James paused, grimacing as he squatted against a tree to rest. They'd been walking, or in his case limping, for the last two hours. He knew if he sat down he might not be able to get up again, but at this point he didn't care. He hurt too much to continue and the shade from the tree brought welcome relief from the broiling sun.

James rubbed his swollen knee and felt the pain extend up his leg, into his back and down into his foot. His face felt like it had gone through a meat grinder and his whole body seemed to be covered in tender bruises that hurt whenever he moved.

"Don't worry. We get there James. We rest now. Good time to rest."

Munny spoke to Chemsi and she relayed the message to the rest of the girls. James watched the two working together. When Munny had told Chemsi about a place he'd heard of that took in girls like them, a place called the Mongoose House, Chemsi had rallied the girls behind the idea. Filled with excitement, they'd all agreed to go, even Shukira.

Since then, Chemsi and Munny had worked together like a tag-team, leading the group through the muddy disaster zone that was now Phnom Penh.

Unable to keep up, James had relegated himself to the back of the pack, dragging his injured knee behind him like a walking zombie.

The night on the rooftop had been a restless one with little sleep. But by morning, the flood waters had receded, leaving a scene of absolute carnage in its wake.

Cars were smashed into buildings, debris was strewn in every direction, and mud was everywhere.

Then there was the smell—the smell of mud, the smell of rot and decay, the smell of dead animals and people.

James leaned his head back against the trunk of the tree and closed his eyes, trying to push the putrid smells and images from his mind. The tree was one of the few he'd seen in the city that hadn't been uprooted by the flood. Its strong limbs were still outstretched with green leaves, providing an almost other-worldly image amidst the chaos.

They'd come across a number of survivors rummaging through the streets and had stopped to help pull a few people from the mud-filled first floors of buildings. On one street corner a crowd had gathered around an old man sitting on the hood of a demolished car. He had a small battery-powered radio that played the voice of a news reporter.

Munny translated for James, and they learned that the storm had produced two known twisters, like tornados, in different parts of the city. The powerful rains and the rare hail storm had overwhelmed the new dam, just as James suspected. The dam's failure caused the Mekong River to flood half of the city.

It's a war zone, James thought. *The place looks like a war zone.*

He took deep breaths and rubbed his swollen knee.

My adrenaline is gone. There's no way I can make this walk. Yesterday, I felt like Superman fighting those guys on the roof, but now I just feel broken and older than ever.

The sound of a helicopter beat in the sky, and James looked up, watching it flying low across the city skyline in their direction. There was no use trying to wave it down. They'd seen a few helicopters flying overhead, but they were filming the disaster, not stopping to help people.

They'd seen a few emergency vehicles on the streets, but they were immediately overwhelmed with survivors seeking help, many carrying their dead and injured loved ones with them.

I shouldn't complain, James scolded himself. *I'm one of the lucky ones. I'm still alive.*

He squeezed his eyes tighter. He was thankful to be alive.

But I can't keep up this pace.

"Munny," he called, waving his friend over.

Friend? James thought. He wondered at the word. He'd only known Munny for a single day, but a bond had been forged between them and James trusted the man. He trusted him with his life.

Yes, he's my friend. Maybe my only friend.

"What is it?" Munny asked. "You okay? No heart attackers, right? I learn CPR on internet. I push chest hard and make beat."

Munny put his hands together and mimicked giving CPR in the air. "Internet say to push to American song, *Staying Alive*. It good song by Bee Gees. You know the song?"

Munny started singing the song as he pumped his hands together in the air. James rolled his eyes and let out a painful chuckle. Even laughing hurt.

"Yes, I know the song, and no, I'm not having a heart attack. And it's attack, not attacker. But I can't walk any further. I'm so dehydrated that I'm not sweating anymore, and my leg is too injured to keep moving. I want you guys to go without me. You and Chemsi keep leading these girls to the Mongoose House. You need to get them there before dark. I worry it won't be safe here when night comes."

Images of Hurricane Katrina and other disasters flashed through James' mind. He'd seen and heard about the looting and problems that came after disasters. He worried what might happen to them if they got caught in the city another night.

"No way, Jose," Munny said, accenting the J incorrectly. "You come with us. You not safe by yourself. We no leave you here."

"I'm slowing you way down. You need to go ahead without me. These girls are more important than I am."

Munny shook his head. "No way, Jo-"

"Don't say it," James cut him off. "It's pronounced Ho-zay, not Joe-say. And where did you learn that phrase anyway? Never mind. Don't tell me. Just get the girls and go. You're burning up daylight."

This time Munny gave James a confused look. "How do you burn the daylight? I not understand."

"Just go!" James shouted. "Leave me here and get them to safety!"

James was yelling, though he wasn't sure why. He knew Munny didn't deserve to be screamed at, but he was tired of arguing. He'd made up his mind and he was not moving from this tree until emergency help came to lift his broken self off the ground.

If help comes at all.

He closed his eyes and started to cry.

I'm going to die here, he thought. *But at least I did something good before I go.*

A small hand rested on top of his and he opened his eyes to find the little girl, Veata, smiling at him.

She tilted her head and spoke a few words in Khmer. Taking both of his hands in hers, she pulled, trying to get him to stand. Her face went red and she grunted, straining to pull up his massive frame.

"What did she say?" James asked Munny, unwilling to move as the girl struggled.

"She says you come with us. If you don't move then she stay, too."

The girl stopped pulling and spoke a few more words.

"She says your colors are dim. And she not leave you alone. She help you walk."

There she is with the colors again, James thought.

He remembered the way she'd talked about his colors on the roof and how he'd seen swirling golden lights emanating from her body. But he chalked that up to hallucinations from the stress of the situation—a psychotic break in reality.

Either way, he knew this little girl was special. There was something about her words that rang true—a simple wisdom he couldn't deny.

Veata tugged on his arms again and grunted, her face turning red.

James shook his hands free from Veata's grip. "Quit it, now. I can't move. I might be able to hobble on my good leg for a bit, but my body's overheating. I'm not sweating anymore and I need water—we all need water."

Munny pursed his lips and looked up at the sky for a few minutes. He turned back to James and smiled. "Okay, James. We rest twenty minutes. If I no get you water by then, we leave you like you ask. But if water come, then so do you. Deal?"

James rested his head back against the tree, letting his full exhaustion set in.

"Is it deal?" Munny asked again.

"Fine. It's a deal. But where are you going to find clean water in this place? It's all a giant mud pit. Your best bet is to get outside the city, get help and get to the safe house. Then send someone back for me."

Munny shook his head. "Twenty minutes. Just wait."

The minutes passed away—five, ten, fifteen. James felt his energy draining like a sieve. His head bobbed to the left and to the right. He wanted to go to sleep and not wake up. But each time he nodded off, Veata pinched his arm and pulled on his beard.

"Veata, let me sleep," James groaned with his eyes still closed. "I just need some rest. I just need a long, peaceful rest."

James felt the girl pinch him again before tugging on his white beard. James didn't respond this time. He was too exhausted and sleep was coming. He was slipping into the gentle void when something wet hit his cheek just below his eye.

His muddled mind stirred back to consciousness. *Did she just spit on me?*

"Veata. Don't do that. Don't spit on people."

Another wet drop hit his face, then another, and another.

His eyes fluttered open and through the openings in the tree branches, he saw gray clouds rolling across the sky. Within minutes, a steady drizzle fell to the ground.

Munny walked into view, holding a bucket he'd found somewhere in the debris. "See! I told you I get water. Monsoon rain come like clockwork. It good water to drink. We fill buckets and drink. Then you feel better."

Veata squeezed James' hand again and smiled before dashing out from under the tree to play in the rain.

A memory from long ago came to mind. He saw his own little daughters playing in the rain, splashing and laughing.

He smiled, forgetting his pain and exhaustion for just a moment.

- 11 -
Friend or Foe

People cheered and danced on rooftops and in the streets as the rain fell from above. Even in the middle of such destruction, their happiness was contagious and Veata couldn't help but join in their excitement—dancing and twirling as the cool drops of liquid fell.

With the rain came thick gray clouds and a reprieve from the miserable afternoon heat. With the rain came a chance for Veata to wash away the mud that was caked across her from head to toe. But most important of all, with the rain came clean water to drink.

Munny handed Veata a small orange bottle he'd scavenged from a pile of trash. She held it in the air to catch the rain, took a drink, and repeated the process over and over again. Staying close to James, she helped him take sips of water and was glad to see his colors grow stronger with each drink.

I think he will be okay, she thought with relief.

She'd been worried about her giant. His colors had faded so much she knew he was giving up and preparing for death. But he'd saved her from the flood and fought for her on the roof. She couldn't let him give up. She had to help him.

The rains continued for another hour and Veata was happy they were normal rains, soft and steady, not like the crazy weather from the day before.

And though the rain cleaned the caked mud from her skin and gave her water to drink, her stomach twisted with hunger. She had not eaten since yesterday, and what little food had been in her stomach she threw up on the man who had tried to kiss her.

"I need some food," Veata heard a girl say. She was sitting in a small group off to the side and her colors were dim and weak.

"Me too," another moaned, her long eyelashes seeming to droop as her blue mascara smeared down her face from the rain. "I'm so hungry. I don't know if I can keep walking. What I wouldn't do for a small cup of rice?"

"Or a big bowl of noodles," another girl added, "with fish covered in green curry gravy."

The group sighed in agreement.

"Even better," said a tall girl with long scar on her shoulder, "How about a giant bowl of sweet jelly in shaved ice and coconut cream."

"Oh yeah," the girls said, nodding.

Veata held her stomach, imagining such delicious food. But thinking about it only made her hunger worse.

"Shut up about food!" Shukira ordered. "We never ate that good back at the brothel. You're only making it worse. Here. Take one of these."

Shukira pulled a handful of wrapped candies from her pocket and held them out to girls.

Their eyes lit up with excitement.

"Where did you get those?" one whispered.

"How many more do you have?"

"Give me one."

"Watch out! That one's mine."

"Hey, what about me? I need one too."

"Stop it," Veata cried as the small group of girls fought over the pieces of candy. "Don't take those. They're bad for you. They'll make you sick!"

But the girls ignored her, fumbling to unwrap the hard candies and shove them into their mouths.

"STOP!" Veata screamed, trying to pull away the candy from the girl with the scar on her shoulder.

The candy slipped free from the girls hand and fell into the mud. The tall girl shoved Veata away and fell to her hands and knees, searching for the candy. Desperately wading her fingers through the mud, she found grasped the hard candy in a fistful of mud, and quickly tossed it into her mouth.

"What's going on?" Chemsi asked, hurrying over. "Why the screaming and the fighting?"

Chemsi helped Veata back to her feet and eyed the rest of the group.

Shukira stood up and held out her hand. "I have one left. Do you want it?"

Veata watched Chemsi's colors flare emerald green. Her eyes went wide and she licked her lips.

"Where did you get it?"

Shukira shrugged. "I always keep a stash on me. I had one already. Do want it?"

Chemsi reached out to take it, but Veata tugged on her dress. "Don't," Veata said. "It's not good. It hurts your colors."

Veata watched the girls who'd taken the candy. All of their colors dimmed to a slate bluish-gray, including Shukira.

Shukira's eyes started to glaze over and she moaned. "This is so much better than food."

Chemsi's lip trembled and she hesitated, looking back at Veata.

"Don't," Veata said, shaking her head, pleading for her to stop.

"I…I can't," Chemsi whispered and she turned back to grab the candy, but it was gone. Another girl had joined the group and snatched it up.

Veata held Chemsi's hand and squeezed it gently, but Chemsi shook her off.

"It's time to walk!" Chemsi barked as she marched back to the front of the group. "The rain is stopping. We have a long way to go. So get up!"

Veata watched Munny come to Chemsi's side, a worried look in his eye. He asked her something, but she just turned her head and stormed away.

Munny looked like he was about to go after her, but stopped and turned to the rest of the group.

"Okay, you heard Chemsi. It's time to go. Carry any water you can in your buckets and bottles. Save it for later and drink sparingly. It has to last all day. The roads are muddy so watch your step and stick together. Does everyone understand?"

Most of girls nodded, while other sat lethargically on the ground. "We can do it," Munny said. "We'll get to the Mongoose House. We just have to keep moving. C'mon. Stand up. Let's go."

After a little more coaxing, all of the girls stood and started walking.

"We go now, James," Munny called to Veata's giant. James raised a hand and nodded, saying something in English.

Munny seemed satisfied with the answer and hurried to the front of the group to catch up to Chemsi.

But when Veata looked back at James, he remained sitting like a stone against the tree.

"Come on. Get up," she said in Khmer, but he didn't respond. She knew he couldn't understand Khmer so she motioned her hands upward, beckoning him to stand. He stayed rooted in place and shook his head, a sad look in his eyes.

This was not a good sign. Veata placed her hands on her hips and huffed. She gave James a hard stare, trying to mimic the look she remembered her mother giving her whenever she was in trouble.

James said something in English and quirked an eyebrow upward.

But Veata didn't relent. She kept staring and held his gaze.

After a few more seconds, the corner of James mouth lifted into a smile and he mumbled something in English, shaking his head.

Placing his large hands on the ground, he tried to push himself up from the base of the tree. After a series of grunts, he only moved a few inches before falling back to the ground.

Breathing heavy from the exertion, his shoulders slumped forward and he looked back at Veata, defeated.

"You must get up, Giant. I will get help."

Veata ran through the group of girls calling for help. "Stop. The giant needs our help. Stop. Please. Come help him. Please."

Though exhausted themselves, some of the girls stopped. Her call for help went up the line until it reached Chemsi and Munny at the front of the pack. Turning around, they came to the tree and surrounded James.

Munny spoke to him in English, and Veata frowned as James shook his head and pointed to his knee and back.

His face was covered in purple bruises, partly hidden by his white beard, and his nose and eye was still swollen from the fight.

"He wants to stay and wait for help. He says we should go without him and get to safety, then come back for him," Munny translated to the group.

"NO!" Veata exclaimed defiantly. "He is my giant. He comes with us. I will help him walk."

Munny smiled and spoke to James, who rolled his eyes and shook his head. But when he looked back at Veata his face softened until he finally nodded, and said, "Okay."

"Okay," Veata repeated, not knowing exactly what the word meant. Soon everyone grabbed a hold of James and pulled. He grimaced as they helped lift his large body into a standing position and the full weight of his bulk pressed against his knees.

Veata found a long, thick branch that had broken off a tree during the flood and dragged it over to James.

"You can use it to walk," she said in Khmer. "I'll stay by your side and help."

James took the stick and leaned against it, testing its strength. After nodding his approval, he patted Veata on the head and said something in English.

"Thank you."

Veata didn't know what "thank you" meant either, but she repeated the newfound English words, letting their foreign sound roll off her tongue.

"Okay, thank you," she replied.

James let out a pained chuckle and tried to take a step forward. Veata watched his colors flare red and blue while his face contorted in pain. He paused, took a deep breath, and then another step.

Veata went to his side and held his free hand in hers. "I'll walk with you. We'll go together."

Muddy step by muddy step, the group moved forward. Often they paused to let James and Veata catch up, refusing to leave them behind. They walked through the streets of Phnom Penh for another hour, passing destruction at every turn.

At one point, Veata was caught off guard when James suddenly tried to cover her eyes with his large hands. But he'd been too slow. She'd seen the woman's dead body on the side of the street, a man and his children kneeling beside her—weeping.

After another hour, Veata's water and that of the other girls, was nearly gone. She offered the final drink to James, but he refused, putting it back up to her lips and forcing her to drink.

The clouds departed and the hot sun was blazing once more. Even worse were the bugs, which came out in full force after the rains. She was used to the mosquitoes, but it was clear her Giant was not. He twitched and slapped and tried to shoo the bugs away, but it was an impossible battle.

They turned the corner at the next street and nearly plowed into the group of girls ahead of them, who'd come to an abrupt stop.

"What's wrong?" Veata asked, trying to get a better look.

A wide-eyed Munny pushed himself back through the group toward herself and James.

Walking beside him were two uniformed police officers that did not look happy.

- 12 -
Michael Jackson

James gritted his teeth when he saw Munny flanked by two officers.

Though their blue uniforms were covered in mud, the batons in their belts and the helmets on their heads made it clear they were police.

"No good," Munny said to James in English. "We not know if they good police or bad."

Munny looked scared to death with the police standing on each side.

"Relax, Munny. Just follow the story we rehearsed and we'll be okay."

Munny nodded and took a deep breath, but he didn't relax.

They'd seen a handful of police officers in the city and worried they might get stopped at some point. It wasn't every day you saw thirty girls in red dresses walking down the street with two men, especially when one of them was a six-foot-eight white guy.

Both James and Munny worried about the police after their run-in with the officer on the roof. So James concocted a cover story that night on the rooftop and Munny helped spread the story among the girls.

They were a girls' choir and James was a foreign choir director visiting Cambodia. While on their way to a performance, the flood hit their bus and they narrowly escaped with their lives.

"You're definitely an author," Munny had commented when James pitched the story.

"It's not my best work, but not too shabby if you ask me," James replied.

The officers looked James up and down, pausing on his face which he knew must be black and blue with the bruises.

The larger of the two cops directed a question toward James, who in turn looked to Munny for a translation.

"He asked if you are James Moore," Munny said in a shaky voice. "I knew you shouldn't have given them your name on the roof. Maybe one of the customers told on us already. Whatever you do, no telling them your real name. Keep secret."

James understood Munny's concern, but something the second officer was doing caught his attention and he ignored Munny's advice.

"Yes, I am the author James Moore," James said, trusting his instincts. "What can I do for you?"

Munny stared at James in disbelief, his mouth wide open. But before he could translate, the officer's grim faces lit into beaming smiles and they started bobbing their heads in excitement. The second officer pushed the first and gave him a look that said, "I told you so."

The big officer gave James a thumbs up and the other one high-fived his partner as they repeated a similar phrase multiple times.

"They say they are huge fans, huge fans, huge fans," Munny translated.

"No kidding. I might have guessed that from the smiles and high fives. Can you ask them for their names?"

The officers' grinned ear-to-ear as they spoke with Munny.

"Big guy on the right is Dith and skinny guy is Po," Munny replied, pointing to each in turn. Both officers greeted James with firm handshake, before pulling him into an awkward hug.

"Okay, boys. Simmer down. It's nice to meet you as well, but I'm not much of a hugger."

Munny just grinned in amazement and continued to translate. "Dith and Po knew you in town for book signing, but they on duty and couldn't come. They really look forward to the next movie. Say it best story and movie they seen in long time."

Officer Po produced a pen and a small pad of paper and practically begged for an autograph. Munny and the girls just stared in disbelief.

"No offense, James, but this happen often? It kind of weird. And how you know they not bad police and arrest us when they walk up?"

"It was a lucky guess," James said while signing the autographs. "I noticed that Officer Po looked a little nervous, fidgeting with a pad of paper and his pen. After signing enough autographs, you start to recognize the fans wanting to ask for one. I took a chance. You're right, though—this is a little weirder than usual, but maybe they can help us out."

After the autographs, the officers seemed to settle down and examined the group of girls with James. In much more controlled, police-like tones, they turned to Munny and started asking questions.

With a fake smile, Munny turned to James to translate. "They want to know if we need any help and why all of these girls are with us. What should I tell them? You no be a choir director now?"

"Just relax Munny. We can essentially stick to the same story. Tell them we were walking the streets after the book signing when the flood hit. We saw a bus full of girls stranded and we helped them escape. We are trying to get them back to their neighborhood north of the city and could use a lift."

Munny raised an eyebrow. "Okay, that not half-bad," he said hesitantly, "but we probably not mention you-know-who's house. They might be in love with you James, but the lady who runs this place has a lot of enemies in city, including police."

James nodded. "Fine. We keep it secret and give them vague directions."

Munny did not look convinced, but he shared the story with Po and Dith. The two listened stoically, looking impressed when Munny finished.

"They say we heroes...like Jerical in your books," Munny translated.

Po and Dith nodded their heads in agreement and repeated the words, "You heroes," in English. They told Munny a friend of theirs owned a small grocery store a few blocks away and had a delivery truck. If it wasn't damaged from the flood, they would try to borrow it and take them where they needed to go.

"That would be wonderful," James said. He wasn't sure how much longer his leg would hold out before he collapsed for good.

The group followed the officers a few blocks east until they arrived at a small store. Leaning on only two wheels against the exterior brick wall of the store, was a beat-up Datsun delivery truck. The truck was pale blue under the coating of mud and it was pinned in place by a small mound of tree limbs, a couch, some shelves, loads of trash, and some poor kid's pink bicycle.

"Well, I don't think we'll be driving anywhere today," James grumbled upon seeing in the wreck.

But officers Po and Dith appeared undeterred by the sight. They spoke in Khmer and Munny translated.

"They think it still run," Munny said. "They go check with owner."

"No way," James scoffed. "If that truck runs then I'm Mary Poppins."

Through the broken glass of the shop, James saw a woman and her teenage son shoveling loads of mud out of the store and back into the street. Po and Dith spoke with the woman and within a minute she and her son were hurrying out the door to meet them. The woman owner ran up to James, shook his hand and spouted off a string of sentences in Khmer. Then, she and her son eagerly worked to clear the debris from around the truck.

"What was that all about?" James asked.

Munny chuckled. "I think owner didn't want to help, but Po and Dith tell her who you are. They promise her you rich American and will help pay for her to fix store if truck works and we can use it."

"What?" James exclaimed, caught off guard.

Po gave James a wink and a thumbs up before calling the girls and Munny over to help clear a path to the truck.

James stood there, still surprised by the bargain the officers had struck with the shop owner, but no less convinced the truck would ever run. His injuries prevented him from being much help, but James watched in amazement as their ragtag crew cleared a path to the truck and helped resettle it so it stood on flat, albeit muddy, ground.

The owner produced a small key ring from her pocket and was about to climb into the driver's seat to try and start it, when James hobbled over to stop her.

"No, no, no," James protested. "Don't try to start it right away. I mean, I doubt this thing will start at all, but if you try it right now, it's dead for sure."

Munny translated and the owner seemed to get upset.

"She say you just try to back out of fixing her store. She says you a liar. She says you—"

James held up a hand to cut him off. "I'm a lot of things, but I'm *not* a liar. Tell her to chill out and pop the hood to the truck. Let me see if I can get it running. And if I do, which is a big *if,* I'll give her enough money to fix her store and then some."

Munny translated and the store owner popped the hood.

James took one look inside at the muddied engine compartment and let out a long sigh. "Well, let's get to work."

Few people knew that James was an absolute gearhead. He'd always fixed his own vehicles since the time he bought his first—a black 1965 Mercury Caliente. Even after he'd gained his wealth as an author, he still found it relaxing to hang out in his garage full of classic cars and dig under the hood every once in awhile.

But the mess in front him seemed an exception to this rule. The owner's son found a stool for him to sit on and brought out a toolbox with some wrenches and a socket set.

James smiled as Veata climbed up the front of the truck and stood on the dented bumper to get a better look. She seemed entranced with the engine and watched intently as he went to work.

"First, we disconnect the battery and check the engine oil," James said. "Good. No water drops on the stick. We don't have to change the oil."

He let Veata wipe the dipstick clean and helped her put it back in place.

Po and Dith came over and frowned when they saw the engine. They spoke to Munny and walked to the back of the truck.

"What'd they say?" James asked.

"They say good luck with that mess. They not know engines very good, but they change the flat tire and clean junk out of truck bed."

James nodded. "Well, none of that's going to matter if I can't get this rig started. Now I've got to check the plugs."

Veata nodded as if she knew what he was talking about and said, "Okay, thank you," causing James to chuckle. He wished he'd taken the time to work on cars with his own kids when they were little. He doubted any of them even knew how to change their own oil.

I've got no one to blame for that except myself.

He'd always hidden in the garage to work on cars. He'd hidden in his office to write.

I just hid from everyone, he thought, and felt a pang of guilt stab him in the heart.

He turned back to Veata. "Okay, you want to help me out?"

Veata nodded her head. "Help. Okay, thank you."

James smiled and patted her on the head. "Good, because I could use a little help right now."

James removed all of the spark plugs, letting Veata examine each of them as she laid them in a row. He left the cylinders of the engine wide open and reconnected the battery.

"Okay, now try to start it up. Let's see if any water got in the engine."

No sooner had the store owner turned the key than dirty brown water shot out of all six cylinders, spraying James and Veata.

Veata made a disgusted face as she spit the dirty water from her mouth and wiped her eyes.

"I think there water in engine," Munny said, safely dry from a few feet away.

"No. You don't say?" James replied, wiping his wet face on his sweaty shirt sleeve.

"Okay, Veata," James said to the girl. "How about we take a few steps back this time while the engine clears out."

Veata nodded. "Help. Okay thank you."

James gave instructions for the owner to turn the key again and give it a little gas. It took another minute, but eventually the water stopped spraying from the engine block.

While James and his little helper reattached the spark plugs and wires, the shop owner and his son slogged back into their muddy shop and up to their apartment above the store.

They returned with some dry rags and a basket of wrapped rice cakes. There were not enough cakes for each person, but the girls shared amongst themselves, devouring their first taste of food in over a day.

James shook his head as Veata tried to share her rice cake with him. He didn't want to take away any food from her or the other girls and insisted she eat it all. But while he was ratcheting the last spark plug in place, the little girl shoved a piece of rice cake into his open mouth.

Though it was only a small bite, James felt a small surge of energy from the morsel of food. He only hoped they would find some more food before night fell.

Using the dry towels, James, Veata, and Munny worked to clean and dry the belts, battery, and engine.

"Okay," James said crossing his fingers in the air.

"Okay," Veata mimicked, crossing her fingers.

He gave the owner a thumbs up and hoped for the best.

The store owner turned the key and the truck squealed and shuddered before falling silent.

The owner tried again with similar results, though this time gray smoke billowed out the exhaust before the engine died.

James was about to swear when he remembered there was still a little eight-year-old girl at his side. The last thing he needed was her repeating American swear words all day like a parrot.

"Try one more time," James called. "But give it a little more gas."

Munny translated and the owner gave it another try. The engine whinnied and moaned until the owner slammed her foot on the gas.

Black smoke shot out of the exhaust. The engine sputtered to life and bawled like a sick kitten, but it was running.

"Woohoo!" Munny shouted. "Way to go, James! You like MacGyver."

James laughed, overjoyed to have the truck running, and surprised by the MacGyver reference.

The girls piled into the back of the canvas covered truck and Munny claimed a seat on the tailgate next to Chemsi. Since there wasn't enough room for James in the back, Po and Dith insisted he squeeze into the cab with them.

But before he could close the door, a little hand grabbed his pant leg and Veata hoisted herself into his lap.

She pointed a finger at him and narrowed her eyebrows. "Okay, thank you," she said sternly.

James laughed. "Well, I can't argue with that."

Munny had given Dith general directions for their location, telling them about a monastery on the outskirts of town where they could be dropped off. He still didn't completely trust the officers and didn't want to tell them their true destination. Besides, Munny said he didn't know exactly where the Mongoose House was, only that it was in the area of the Monastery.

"We ask monastery for direction. They should know where it is. But I no trust police," Munny had said. He also warned James to keep his eyes open for trouble, or rather, he said, "Keep eyes big for bad things."

The truck pulled away from the store slowly, occasionally sliding a bit on the muddy streets, but they made steady progress through the back half of the city. The language barrier proved difficult at first and James had no way to communicate with the officer. That is until Po found a cassette tape of Michael Jackson in the glove compartment.

Popping in the tape and turning up the music, Po sang along to *Beat It* in near-perfect English. Dith joined the solo and turned it into a duet. By the time the second chorus came around, James couldn't help himself and the duet morphed into a choir as James added his baritone voice.

Veata bobbed her head to the music and swayed her shoulders as the three sang along. After the song finished, the trio looked at each other and broke into laughter. They had found a way to communicate.

It was slow moving through the damaged streets, but James was thankful to rest his body. They reached the outskirts of the city as the sun started to set and James recognized the description of the monastery that Munny had given him. To his left, a short stone wall with faded red paint appeared as it stretched along the side of the road. A building stood back amongst a grove of trees and an arched entryway with white gate could be seen further ahead.

"You can stop here," James said, pointing to the gates of the monastery.

Dith just smiled and kept driving as he and Po continued to sing.

"Stop here, Dith," James said more forcefully, pointing at the gates as they passed. "That's the monastery. We need to go there. Stop the truck!"

Dith said something back in Khmer, and Po replied. The two briefly yelled at each other, ignoring James, and Dith turned onto a small country road and kept driving.

James tensed, wondering what to do.

Should I grab the steering wheel? I can't overpower both of them in this confined place. And if I try, everyone in the back could get seriously hurt. And what about Veata. She's too close and could get hurt.

He eyed their holstered guns and worried that he'd seriously misjudged the two officers. His mind raced through the worst possible scenarios. *What if they work for the Sen Zi and they're just moving the girls to another location? What if they kill us? How do I warn Munny? Maybe he can fight them off...but what about their guns?*

Dith turned down another dirt road just as the sun disappeared over the horizon. He flipped on the headlights as the intro to *Thriller* started to play.

The whole moment felt surreal as Dith and Po sang along.

This is like some weird movie, James thought, starting to doubt his sanity. *This doesn't happen in real life. This is all too crazy. It can't be real.*

But then James felt Veata squeeze his hand. She looked up into his eyes, and he knew this was real. He knew he had to protect them.

He was just about to slam an elbow into the side of Po's head and try to reach the brakes, when Dith started to brake on his own. The truck rolled to a stop and the headlights lit up some small buildings in a field surrounded by a tall barbed-wire fence.

Is this a prison? James panicked.

He had no idea where they were, and quickly scooped Veata into his arms and flung open the front door. The song to Thriller continued to play in the background as James limped to the back of the truck and nearly collided with Munny, who looked equally alarmed.

"Did they take us to prison?" James asked. "This does not look good."

"I—I don't know," Munny stammered. "I never been here before. I said stop at monastery. Why they not stop? Why you not tell them?"

"I did!" James exclaimed. "I tried to tell them but they wouldn't listen. They both have guns. I don't think we can fight them."

Dith and Po whistled to the tune of *Thriller* as they stepped out of the truck. James set Veata down on the truck bed and took off his belt to use as a weapon, preparing for the worst.

Munny anxiously whispered for the girls to huddle together in the back of the truck and he climbed onto the tailgate, ready to pounce on the officers.

But just before the officers rounded the corner, Munny shook James' shoulder and pointed to a sign about thirty feet away behind the barbed wire fence. He exhaled a sigh of relief.

"It okay," Munny said, pointing to the sign written in Khmer. "It say *Welcome to Mongoose House.*"

- 13 -

Mongoose House

Veata devoured her meal of steaming soup and rice. Unlike the soups she'd always made for her uncle, this soup wasn't thin and watery. Thick with seasonings, mixed vegetables, and pieces of tender chicken, it was the best soup she had ever had. In fact, it was the best meal she'd ever had.

"I think our young guest likes the soup," a kindly woman said with a smile. Her name was Boupha Mam, the founder of the Mongoose House.

Veata was entranced by Boupha's dazzling colors. They encircled the older woman with bright orange flames and shimmering gold threads that flowed throughout a dark blue.

After arriving at the Mongoose House, Boupha had not only opened her doors to welcome the girls, but she'd opened her arms, giving each girl a hug while whispering a kind word in their ear.

There were dozens of other girls and boys, along with some older men and women at the home. With practiced precision, they worked together to set up tables in a large dining area and quickly prepared soup and rice for the newcomers.

Boupha had invited Chemsi, Munny, and James to sit with her and share their tale as they ate. Veata had refused to leave James' side and nestled herself between James and Boupha on the bench.

After licking her bowl clean, Veata let out a loud burp, causing the others at the table to chuckle.

"Would you like more soup?" Boupha asked with a wink.

Veata nodded eagerly and licked her lips.

"Hey, save some for the rest of us," Chemsi joked.

Veata's eyes went wide and she looked down, embarrassed. "Is there not enough?" Veata asked. "I'm sorry. I don't have to eat anymore. The others need it more than me."

Boupha, Chemsi, and Munny all chuckled again. The only one not laughing was James who looked confused until Munny spoke to him in English. He smiled at Veata and gave her a side hug.

"You are a very sweet girl," Boupha spoke softly. "We have plenty of soup available for everyone. Please, eat your fill. This is your new home. Our food is your food."

Veata felt warmth rush to her cheeks and she dipped her head to Boupha. "Is it really our home?" she asked. "Can I really stay?"

Boupha laid a hand on Veata's shoulder and pulled her close. "Of course, child. You can stay. You are safe here. You are loved here."

Veata's eyes swelled with tears and she wrapped her small arms around Boupha's waist and buried her face in Boupha's lap. It had been a long time since she had felt safe. It had been a long time since she had felt loved. She had not heard those words since her mother and father passed away, and she'd forgotten how good it felt to hear them.

Pulling back from Boupha, she wiped her eyes against the sleeve of her ragged red dress. "And what about my giant? Can he stay, too? Can James stay with us?"

Boupha turned to James, a hint of a smile on her face. "Veata wants to know if her giant can stay with us," she said in perfect English. "You are welcome to stay as long as you like, Mr. James, or should I call you Veata's Giant?"

- 14 -
Lullaby

"Shall I sing you a goodnight lullaby?" James asked as he tucked Veata into the white sheet on her sleeping mat.

Veata smiled and repeated the word, "lullaby," followed with "Okay, thank you."

James coughed, clearing his throat, and sang.

Oh, I had such a pretty dream, Mama.
Such pleasant and beautiful things
Of a dear little nest, in the meadows of rest
Where the birdie her lullaby sings.
Of a dear little nest, in the meadows of rest
Where the birdie her lullaby sings.

Veata smiled, her eyes growing heavy as he continued.

A stream sang and flowed on toward the ocean
Thro' shadows and pretty sunbeams
Each note grew more deep, and I soon fell asleep
And was off to the Island of Dreams
Each note grew more deep, and I soon fell asleep
And was off to the Island of Dreams

Six other girls shared the small room with Veata. They were all around her age and seemed entranced by his song. From the corner of his eye he could tell they were staring, but whenever he chanced to look at them directly, they diverted their eyes and fidgeted in their beds.

To think what they've suffered, especially at the hands of men. It's no wonder they can't look me in the eye.

Suddenly, James felt guilty for even being in their room. Then, he heard one of the girls softly humming to the chorus as he sang. A second girl gently swayed her head to the music, and his guilt left. In some small measure, the music seemed to build a bridge between them.

I saw there a beautiful angel
With crown all bespangled with dew
She touched me and spoke, and I quickly awoke
And found there, dear Mama, 'twas you
She touched me and spoke, and I quickly awoke
And found there, dear Mama, 'twas you

James gave Veata's hand a gentle squeeze and she squeezed back, a look of complete peace on her face. He started to pull himself up, but his knee buckled under him and he nearly toppled over. Using the corner of an old dresser for support, he gritted his teeth and forced himself to stand.

Part of him wished he'd not kneeled down to tuck Veata into bed. But that thought, and his pain, was pushed aside when Veata whispered, "Okay, thank you, James."

"You're welcome, Veata," he replied.

"You're...welcome," she repeated, her eyelids drooping.

James limped to the door and stopped, turning for one more look at the child that had saved him in so many ways. "Good night," he whispered.

"Good nig—" Veata copied, but the last word fell short as her eyes closed and she dozed off to sleep.

"That was beautiful song," Boupha said from outside the doorway, surprising James.

"Um, thank you. My mom used to sing it to my sisters and me when we were kids."

"Did you sing it to your own children as well?" Boupha asked.

James gave a sad smile. "Not as much as I should have."

Boupha nodded, seeming to understand.

The two walked in silence as they exited the small building that housed a half-dozen small rooms. Stepping into the open air, James was met by a brilliant night sky with thousands of twinkling stars. He found himself feeling small and insignificant as he stared at the lights above.

"You know, we were so busy telling you our story at dinner," James said, "that I didn't have a chance to ask you many questions."

Boupha smiled as they walked across a courtyard toward the main building where they'd had dinner. "And what questions do you have for an old woman like me?"

James shook his head and laughed, remembering too late how laughing hurt bruised ribs and stomach.

"M'am, if you're old, then I'm ancient. But even an ancient old goat like me still has questions. The things I've seen over the last twenty-four hours have seriously changed me forever."

"Have they changed you for the better?" Boupha asked.

James paused as they neared the main building. "Yes, it's changed me for the better. That girl, Veata, she...she is something special. I thought I was saving her and the other girls, but they also saved me in more ways than one."

Boupha nodded sagely. "Do you see the sign on that tree?"

James squinted his good eye since the other one was practically swollen shut, and saw a sign nailed into the trunk of the tree about six feet high. It was green with white Khmer lettering painted on it.

"I see it. What does it say?"

"It's an old Buddhist proverb. There is one hanging from every tree in our sanctuary. That one says, *"Light dispels darkness. Wisdom dispels ignorance.* You helped bring the girls to light. And in so doing, gained wisdom."

James nodded. "That may be, but I still feel pretty ignorant—more than ever in my life. And that's where my questions come in."

Boupha nodded for him to continue.

"First, what's going to happen to these girls? There must be hundreds more like them in the city. How do we free them? I want to know what this place is—your Mongoose House. Why is it called the Mongoose House? What do you do here? Why does it look like a prison on the outside with the razor wire and armed guards? Why did you start this place? And lastly, where did you learn to speak English so well? You speak it better than Munny, but don't tell him I said so."

Boupha chuckled at the last comment and motioned for him to sit with her on a log bench below another tree.

"Those are many questions, Mr. James. I will try to answer them all for you. First, I was sold to a brothel by my mother. I was only a few years older than Veata at the time, but my mother needed money to feed my younger siblings. I was sacrificed for them."

James shook his head in disgust, but Boupha continued.

"I tried to escape twice and was recaptured. I've had a gun pointed at my head, I've been beaten, burned, and I've been locked in a cage where buckets of snakes were thrown on me as a punishment. I saw my friends die. I wanted to die myself. I know what these girls and boys went through. I was drugged, just like them, and beaten into submission.

"When I was sixteen I escaped, but was captured by a policeman who then sold me to another brothel. I was there for two more years until I met a man named Gregory. He was a regular customer and a wealthy foreigner from England. He bought me from the brothel and I lived with him in his vacation villa near the coast."

"And he kept you as a slave?" James growled. He felt the anger swelling inside again, but Boupha rested a hand on his arm and shook her head.

"He kept me as a lover, yes, but I was free to leave and was given money to spend for food and clothing. Though I could have left, I stayed since I had nowhere else to go. I lived there for ten years. Gregory often travelled back and forth to England during that time and even hired me a private tutor to teach me English. While in Gregory's home, we only spoke English. That's how I came to learn the language so well."

"But, what happened? What changed so that you decided to leave?"

"I didn't leave," came Boupha's quick reply. "Gregory left. He sold his home and went back to England for good. He said it was time for him to find a wife and to marry. He left me a large sum of money, all of my clothing, and then he was gone."

"I'm...I'm sorry," James said. "I know how badly it hurts when someone you love leaves you."

Boupha shook her head emphatically and scoffed. "I did not *love* him. He was kinder than most, and I used the money he left to start the Mongoose House, but I never loved him. To be honest, after my experiences in the brothels, I think it's impossible for me to have any romantic feelings of love at all."

James winced at his foolishness. "I apologize. Of course it would be impossible," he said. "I'm trying to compare when my wife left me to your experience, but they're nothing alike. I'm sorry."

Boupha waved a hand in the air. "No, no, do not be sorry. You're just trying to make sense of this new, dark world. Pain afflicts us all. And do not apologize. I have come to peace with my past, as these children must do if they are to survive and live a happy life."

James shuddered as he thought of Veata on her own, out in the dark world by herself. "And how long will they stay?"

"You're thinking of Veata, aren't you?" Boupha asked. "I can see it in your eyes. She is lucky she found her giant. But you need not worry about the child. All of our guests are welcome to stay as long as they wish. Some of the girls leave after only a few days and sneak back to brothels. For some, we are able to locate family members to take them in. But we only do that after extensive research so we know they can be trusted. Then we follow up each month to check on the child and help as needed.

"The others stay here. We teach them to read and write, basic math, music, and the trade of a seamstress. Many of our children leave in their late teens and find work as a seamstress. With their skills they can support themselves and it keeps them from going back to their old lives."

"But why would they want to go back?" James asked, his voice rising, disgusted at the thought.

Boupha laid her palms open in a placating gesture. "For many it's the drug addiction. For others, it's what they've known most of their lives."

James pictured Veata again, and fear wrapped around his thoughts. "Well, can't you just keep them here and force them to stay? You've got the barbed wire fence and armed guards. Just make them stay until they're detoxed and mature enough to leave! This place is clean and safe. Just keep them here until they're ready!"

James took a deep breath, realizing that he'd been shouting.

"I'm sorry for yelling," he said, dropping his face into his hands. "I just, I can't imagine letting them go back to that life."

Boupha shook her head. "I will not force any of the children over fourteen years of age to stay. The young ones rarely try to leave, but if the older teens desire it, they may go. This place is not a prison. I am not their owner. If I force them to stay then I am no better than the brothels."

"What?" James yelled in surprise. "Then why the fences? The armed men? Of course you're better than the brothels! I can't believe you just let them leave. Why would you do that?"

Boupha mumbled something in Khmer and then spoke again in English. "You foolish Americans. Always thinking you know what's best. I have the fence and guards to keep the traffickers out! Fifteen years ago, one of the Sen Zi traffickers came here while I was gone on errands to the city. They shot two adults who help me here and kidnapped sixty-three girls!"

James watched Boupha shaking as she spoke. "The adults survived the shooting, but we never found those girls again. They were shipped off to other cities and countries. I made a promise to myself and these children that I would never allow that to happen again. I found policemen, honest police like Po and Dith, to help. They come to volunteer here as guards. Many of them lost sisters and mothers to the brothels. They help me free other children and I do all I can to protect them."

James was stunned by the revelation.

To lose sixty-three girls like that. I don't think I could handle that and stay sane. But...it still doesn't explain why she lets the others go.

"If you're trying to protect them," James said slowly, gritting his teeth. "Why let them leave to go back to the brothels?"

Boupha closed her eyes and a tear ran down her cheek. "Do you think I want them to leave? Of course not. I talk and plead with them to stay. I do all I can to convince them to stay, but if they want to go, I *must* let them. I have no legal right to keep them here. And I assure them they are always welcome to come back to us. I do my best to keep track of where they go and help them from the outside, but I *will not* take away their freedom to choose. That, I refuse."

James turned his head and he ran a hand through his hair in frustration.

"You must understand what the people of Cambodia have endured," Boupha said in a calmer voice. "Hundreds of thousands were killed in civil war during the 80's. Those that survived were forced to follow the Khmer Rouge regime. There was so much death, so much despair, and so little freedom. I can't take away their freedom."

James sighed. He understood why she allowed the girls to leave, but the thought of them going back to their old way of life made him physically ill.

"It is flooded water that makes mud. It is clear water that cleanses," Boupha said.

James turned back to her, narrowing his brow in confusion.

"Fitting, don't you think?" She continued. "It's the saying above us on this tree. I know it upsets you that I allow them to leave, but it is the right way. These children have been forced into the mud and dirt. I teach and love them as my own. I give them clear water to clean away their past and to try and help them find happiness. I try to give them hope and a new life. But in the end, they must choose. We all must choose. I will not take away their freedom to choose."

James took a few deep breaths and sighed, letting his emotions cool. "I get it. I don't like it...but I get it."

They sat in silence for a time, watching the stars. James' whole world had been turned upside down in a single day. He felt guilty that he, a college-educated father and wealthy, pseudo-celebrity had no clue about the realities of child slavery before this day. He had heard about it in blips on the news, but it always felt so distant and so small. But now, things were different. He was different.

"I want to help," James said matter-of-factly. "I have money. I can buy girls from the brothels, like Gregory bought you. Then take them here where they are safe. We can free hundreds of girls. We can start tomorrow."

Boupha rolled her eyes. "There you go again. Trying to be the hero white man coming to save the day like in the movies, thinking you know best without knowing anything."

James reeled back, confused and a little offended. "What are you talking about? So just because I'm a white foreigner, I can't help? That's all I want to do. I want to free all of the children forced into slavery. I just want to help."

Boupha sighed. "I know. I'm sorry. But I've seen men like you before. They try to come and fix things— foreigners with no clue. And usually, they just make matters worse. You've done much good today and put your life in danger to save these girls. The way your actions caused the girls to rally behind you and fight back—I've never seen or heard of anything so amazing, especially from girls so beaten and brainwashed into submission.

"You are a hero, Mr. James. And I applaud your desire to help. But if we buy freedom for a girl, the traffickers will only fill their brothels with a new child. They will make more money from you, and money from the new child. That method will only give the Sen Zi more power and wealth. It will be a never ending cycle."

"Then how do we fix things? How do we stop this madness?"

"We work with the honest police. We build relationships in the government so laws are enforced and corruption overpowered. We build public support and teach young men to stay out of the brothels. And when we raid the brothels with the police on our side, the owners and their men are arrested, tried, and sentenced to prison. Without punishment, the traffickers are free to continue. This is the only way."

James felt like he'd been sidelined in one of his college football games. He was raring and ready to take action, to go fight and save all of the children in a week, tops. Knowing that it was impossible, and that each day there were children kept as slaves in brothels, hurt. It hurt hard.

"What can I do to help? I have to do something."

Boupha smiled. "There is much you can do, Mr. James. So very much. Come, let us go inside and I will show you to your room. You have had a very long day and I can see the exhaustion in your face. We can discuss our partnership in more detail tomorrow. But for now, you must rest."

James felt the weariness in his body and knew she was right. He knew he had a new mission in life to protect these children. And he would do all he could to help.

Boupha lent her hand to James as he struggled to rise from the bench. Together they walked to the main building, but just before they entered, James saw a pile of dirty, ragged, red dresses piled on the ground outside the door.

He paused and looked at the crumpled garments. "What will you do with those?"

Boupha picked up one of the dirty dresses by the straps and held it in the air. "You asked why I named this place the Mongoose House. I chose it because a mongoose can be a loving creature, yet fierce in the eye of danger. These are qualities these children must have to survive. Love and fierceness.

"Tomorrow we will hold an official welcome ceremony for the new girls. There will be food, introductions, and games. At night we will gather around a large fire in the courtyard. I will tell them my story, much of which I've just shared with you. Then…"

Boupha trailed off and threw the small red dress back into the pile with the others. "We will burn these dresses. The girls will throw them into the fire and their new lives will begin."

THE TALE OF THE MONGOOSE
A *30 RED DRESSES* SHORT STORY

I wonder if he will remember it's my birthday? Veata thought, unable to prevent a smile from spreading across her face.

Today is a good day. Today, I am sixteen.

Veata walked down the hallway from her room to the kitchen. She'd been allowed to sleep in on her birthday, but the smell of fresh eggs and curry rice roused her from bed. Dozens of girls and boys were helping cook alongside Boupha Mam, Chemsi, and Munny. Their colors danced between yellow, green, pink, and blue as they worked together to prepare the morning meal.

It had been eight years since she'd arrived at the Mongoose House on the outskirts of Phnom Penh in Cambodia. Entering the kitchen, she reminisced about the first day she'd come to the gates of the property—thirty girls in red dresses with a Cambodian man and a white giant who was ready to collapse.

Remembering that day, and the devastating flood, brought back a mix of painful and happy memories. Veata felt such pain for the loss of life and destruction that came from the flood. But without it, she and her sisters would still be prisoners of Rithisak, rotting in his brothel until they died.

After arriving at the Boupha Mam house, Veata struggled with her past, as did all of the children who came there. Her gift of colors proved to be a great blessing as she sorted through her own painful memories and helped the other children. As she grew older, she became the unofficial counselor at the Mongoose House. She would spend much of the day listening to the fellow survivors who wished to talk. Many came to her naturally, gravitating toward Veata as she sensed their moods and their inner-most feelings. They unloaded their burdens and she listened, giving them all the support and love she could offer.

Boupha recognized her gift and often sent the new children to visit her when they arrived. Often by the third visit, they started to drop their protective shells and open up to Veata. It was the beginning of their healing process and Veata cherished the work she was doing.

Her friendship with Chemsi grew stronger as they lived together in the Mongoose House. Chemsi reminded Veata of Boupha. They were both natural leaders, survivors, and determined to help other children escape the brothels.

Chemsi soon became Boupha's right-hand woman over the operation. Veata became the healer.

But living at Boupha Mam's was not free of danger.

Veata chuckled to herself when she remembered her first impressions of the place after they'd arrived. The property was surrounded by high metal fences with barbed wire lined across the top. Two armed guards patrolled the two acre parcel of land 24/7, and from the outside it looked like a prison.

But Veata had learned of the past sadness Boupha had endured when sixty-three girls were kidnapped from the home by the Sen Zi. It was for this reason the fences and guards were employed. They were not to keep the girls in, but to keep the traffickers and the brothel men out.

Boupha had spent years searching for those missing girls, using every means and contact she had available to find them, but they were never found.

Occasionally, in the early morning dawn, Veata would catch Boupha sitting by herself under the mango tree, staring at the tall gated entrance to their sanctuary. Dark blue colors would fall around her like rain and she would sing to herself a song from the dark days of the Khmer Rouge regime.

They took my land
My sorrow grows
They took my home
My sorrow grows
They took my freedom
My sorrow grows
They took my children
My sorrow is full

Veata imagined the absolute heartbreak Boupha must have endured with such a great loss. She loved these children as her own.

After the mass kidnapping, Boupha vowed to never let anything like it happen again. She went to great lengths to secure the home with fencing, razor wire, and her own private security team made from off-duty police officers she could trust.

But more than giving them a place of protection, Boupha wanted the children to learn to protect themselves. When she heard of Munny's exploits on the roof that fateful day, and that he was a practicing Bokator master, she pleaded with Munny to train the children and the staff.

Bokatar was an ancient Cambodian martial art. Practicing or teaching the fighting style had been outlawed by the Khmer Rouge government for decades so as not to train rebels who would fight against them.

But within the last ten years, Bokatar had been legalized. Munny was more than eager to help train them. Like James, he wanted to help in any way possible. But he had more than one reason for coming back to the Mongoose House each week. Whenever he and Chemsi were around one another, both of their colors would flare soft pink and yellow.

When Chemsi turned twenty-one, the two married.

It was a beautiful wedding, full of colors, laughter and happiness. Even her giant, James Moore, flew from America to attend the wedding as Munny's best man.

My giant, Veata thought, still wondering if he remembered her birthday. Every year he sent a package full of gifts, toys, candies, and books. But lately he'd been so busy as a spokesperson for the United Nations' efforts against human trafficking, his new book tour, fundraisers for the Mongoose House, and visits with his other grandchildren, that she wondered if he'd forgotten this year.

Thanks to James' support, the Mongoose House Charities had grown to sixteen locations covering Cambodia, Thailand, and Laos. They received substantial funding and support from the United Nations in addition to many of James' celebrity friends.

Hundreds of girls and boys were being freed from brothels each year, and the traffickers were being arrested and sentenced to prison.

Things are changing, Veata thought as she took a seat on a stool in the corner of the kitchen.

"Ah, Veata, you're awake," Boupha called as a gaggle of children swarmed around her. Many seemed to be hindering Boupha more than helping as they finished preparing breakfast. "Happy birthday to you, my child! A package arrived for you this morning."

Boupha nodded her head toward a brown box perched on the countertop.

"He remembered!" Veata squealed.

Munny laughed. "Of course he remembered. He may be a grumpy old man, but he will never forget your birthday—never. You're like a grandchild to him. He loves you too much to forget."

"Speaking of child," Chemsi said, pausing her cooking to hold her swollen belly. "This daughter of yours seems to be practicing bokatar in there."

Munny beamed with pride. "Good job, Princess," he whispered, rubbing Chemsi's tummy. "Just don't hurt Mommy, okay."

Veata smiled at the two and grabbed the box off the counter. She was surprised by how light it felt, especially for such a big box. Bringing it to a table in the dining hall, she opened the package, only to find a single envelope nestled in the midst of a foot deep of packing paper.

Curious, she carefully peeled open the sealed envelope. Inside was a long letter addressed to her.

My Dear Veata,

It has been too long since I last visited. Boupha tells me you are doing well with your studies and desire to go to school to be a counselor. I know you will be great at it. You're wise beyond your years and have been blessed with many great gifts.

She also tells me what a beautiful young woman you've become and that the boys are beginning to notice. Just let those boys know that your giant doesn't approve of them noticing too much.

Not that it matters. Munny tells me you're his star pupil in Bokatar lessons. According to him, you can take pretty good care of yourself. Their news and your emails bring me so much joy. Thanks to you, I'm a better man and a better father. My oldest daughter Lilia just had her third child. That's my sixth grandbaby, not including you. You make seven and you're just as dear to me, Veata.

You're probably wondering why there are no gifts in this package. I know we often write each other emails, but I wanted to send you something special this year for your sixteenth birthday.

So instead of treats and other gifts, I decided to write you a story. This story is yours to keep, or yours to share. Personally, I hope you share it with the other children. Maybe that's just my ego as a writer. But I leave it to you.

When I first met Boupha, I asked her why she called the place the Mongoose House. It seemed such an odd name to me at the time. But she simply told me "it is because they can be a loving creature, yet fierce in the eye of danger."

This thought stuck with me and ever since I've had a short story brewing in my head. Finally,

with your birthday approaching, I decided to
write it as a gift—The Tale of the Mongoose.

Once upon a time, venomous cobras roamed an abundant land and terrorized the mice in their domain. New mice would come from miles around seeking food and water in the luscious landscape, only to be trapped by the cunning serpents.

One day, a baby mouse found herself in this predicament by no fault of her own. She'd been born at sea, stowed with her parents in a cage and cared for by a man with large spectacles and bushy blond eyebrows.

After weeks at sea, a fierce storm arose. It whipped the sea into such a fury that mountainous waves crashed over the ship, seeming to swallow it whole.

As the ship listed to right, about to topple over, the man opened their cage to set them free, giving them a chance to survive. The large ship creaked and moaned as the icy salt water ripped it apart and pulled it down into the great fathoms below. In the chaos, the baby mouse was separated from her parents and cast afloat on a splintered piece of wood.

She survived the wicked storm. She survived hunger and thirst. She survived seven hot days and long nights alone on the ocean. Then a miracle occurred. In the distance, a piece of land came into view. The little mouse knew she must reach the land to survive. Dipping her little feet into the water, she kicked and kicked for hours.

Just as her legs felt as if they could kick no longer and the sun began to set, the tide pulled in her piece of wood. It carried the little mouse on gentle waves until she landed softly on a sandy white beach.

The next day, a kind mouse family discovered her on the beach and took her in to raise as their own. The little mouse loved her new family, but it did not take long for her to discover the terrors of the cobras.

She watched in horror as many of her friends and siblings were taunted, trapped, and devoured by the serpents. As time went on, the little mouse grew larger and stronger than all of the other mice. The chief cobra took notice of her growth, greedily eyeing her plump figure.

"She will make a fine meal," the chief told the other cobras. "Tomorrow, let's play with her in the jungle and then let us feast."

When the little mouse left the safety of home to search for food, the snakes made their move. They slithered in a wide arc, flanking her from the back and sides. Before she realized what was happening, they surrounded her in a small clearing and backed against the trunk of a large tree.

"Hello, Mousey. Where are you off to in such a hurry?" the chief cobra hissed.

Trembling against the tree, the mouse fought to stand up tall and face her hunters. "I'm...I'm only gathering food for my family."

The serpent laughed and hissed. "What a

coincidence. I was coming to gather your family for my food."

The chief was too hungry to play with his dinner any longer. His oval shaped hood spread out behind his head and he revealed a terrible set of long, sharp, venomous fangs.

In the blink of an eye, the serpent lunged at the mouse. But just as its fangs were about to find their mark, something triggered deep inside the mouse and she instinctively dodged the attack.

The serpent screamed in frustration, lashing out with another attack. But the mouse knew what to do. It easily avoided strike after strike from the cobra. It dodged left, right, and jumped in the air.

Each time the cobra missed, the mouse found herself less and less afraid of the beast. Instead of trembling in fear, her muscles tightened in anticipation. Her senses were razor sharp and she knew it was time to attack.

With reflexes quick as lightning, the mouse jumped on the back of the cobra. It dug its teeth in the widespread hood of the chief. Too stunned to retreat, the snake shook its head in an attempt to free himself from the mouse.

But his attempts were in vain. The mouse raked her claws into his hood and held fast as she bit and tore into the snake's head and neck.

The other cobras looked on with horror and began to slither away in fear. As life ebbed from the bloodied snake, the chief cobra realized too late that this was no mouse. This was a long lost enemy—one that had disappeared from their lands long ago. This was a mongoose.

> *I hope you enjoyed the story, Veata. You are like this Mongoose, more powerful and strong than you know. You're full of so much love and loyalty, yet there's a fierceness inside of you that I know will keep you safe and allow you to protect others.*

> *And now for your final birthday gift. I have one more surprise that I've been keeping a secret for months—a special song, just for you.*

Veata looked up from the letter, confused. "What does he mean, a song?"

But just as she spoke, a familiar baritone voice filled the air.

> *Oh, I had such a pretty dream, mama.*
> *Such pleasant and beautiful things*
> *Of a dear little nest, in the meadows of rest*
> *Where the birdie her lullaby sings.*
> *Of a dear little nest, in the meadows of rest*
> *Where the birdie her lullaby sings.*

Veata turned to find her giant standing in the doorway, a huge grin on his face.

"Come here little one, and give your grandfather a hug."

Without any hesitation, Veata rushed into James' open arms and held him tight. Together they wept as their colors blossomed into a cascade of brilliant light.

AUTHOR NOTE

On February 11, 2010, my wife came across the website www.Love146.org, a non-profit fighting against human trafficking. I started digging through their website for more information and I came across a video titled, "Imagine." This video didn't just grab me—it shook me. This was my call to action and I knew I had to join the cause for freedom.

You can watch the video here, https://vimeo.com/7473554, but be prepared. This video was the basis for Veata's story.

Watching the video was one of those turning points in my life. I had two little girls at the time (I have five children now), and this video kept me up through the night. I thought of my own children and thought about what I would do to save them from such an awful fate. I imagined the millions of other children suffering as child slaves around the world and it broke my heart. I remember thinking, *If only I could free these kids and adopt them as my own. Give them the protection and the love that all children deserve.*

I had to do something and I decided to get involved. First, I studied. I checked out every book I could find at the library about modern slavery, (aka human trafficking). I read online, visited organization websites, and I started communicating with a handful of people who worked at different NGO's (Non-Governmental Organizations) such as Love146, Free The Slaves, Not For Sale, and the International Justice

Mission. My eyes were opened to the various forms of slavery around the world—sex slavery, child soldiers, rug looms, brick kilns, rubber plantations, cocoa farms, domestic servitude, bonded labor, fishing boats, copper mines, gold mines, diamond mines, and the list goes on.

Next, I started a blog on the subject and built a social media following to help spread awareness and to help gather petition signatures aimed at changing laws in the U.S.A. and abroad. Many of these laws called for stricter punishments against traffickers, and to provide mental and physical aid to trafficking survivors. I volunteered at local events and helped raise a fair amount of money for NGO's. As a blogger, I was even invited to interview trafficking survivors at the Freedom Awards in Los Angeles. I also interviewed celebrities on the red carpet for the awards show, which was way out of my wheelhouse as I was placed next to a dozen other professional news and TV organizations on the red carpet. I had absolutely no clue what I was doing, but I jumped in there and faked it the best I could as I used my phone for a recording device.

Still, I wanted to do more. Most of the books I had read on the subject were heartbreaking and left with me in such a depressed state that I almost wanted to ignore the problem and move on with life...almost. Instead, I decided to try my hand at writing a fictional story about a child trafficking victim. I wanted to get the basic information across about the situations these children face, but make the story palpable with a positive ending of hope.

This turned into the first novel I ever wrote, a book titled *Abolere* (later called *Blackstone*). I learned so much as I wrote this story. For starters, I learned that I loved writing. It was addictive, inspiring, and I found a new passion I didn't know existed within myself. Secondly, I learned quite a bit about story structure, world building, character development, etc...

But the *Abolere* and *Blackstone* stories quickly went off the rails, turning into a mix of the TV show *Psych*, with some *Ironman*, and a hint of *MacGyver*. If you think that sounds awesome, parts of it really were. But this strange mashup was out of control and I knew it wasn't a publishable story. I chalked the experience up to great practice, and tucked the trunk novel away where it would never be seen again.

But boy was I bitten by the writing bug. Story ideas seemed to pop into my head every day. I started keeping a list of book ideas on an excel spreadsheet (something I still do) and I went to work turning these ideas into the written word. After a few more years and four published books, Veata and James' story kept calling back to me. I was in the beginnings of the third book in the *I Am Sleepless* series, but I couldn't shake Veata and James. In February of 2017, I finally decided to pause my work on the *I Am Sleepless* series and dive back into what is now known as *30 Red Dresses*.

I hacked the original story to pieces, cutting it down to the barebones. Then came a complete remodel of the plot and characters. One of the bigger twists I added was Veata's "gift of colors." I wanted a way to show how children can sense the emotions of those around them, yet still be overly trusting and innocent.

In my own mind, I often associate emotions with specific colors. I do the same with musical notes and songs. Maybe it's my inclination toward fantasy and science fiction, but when the idea for Veata's colors came out on the page, I ran with it. But I didn't want to turn this story into a full-blown fantasy with a magic system and powers (though I'll admit, I had some ideas in that direction). I really wanted to keep it grounded in the real world. I worried about adding this twist with the colors, but as I looked at it in revisions, it just felt right to keep it. I feel it adds to the story instead of taking away from it.

One other major change was the length of the story. I opted to make it a shorter novella instead of a full-length novel. I wanted the story to hit hard and quick, but not linger too long on the painful situations of the characters. This was part of my goal to write a hard-hitting story that shared truths about human trafficking, but was palpable and left the reader with hope.

Some have asked if the Mongoose House is a real place in Cambodia. To my knowledge there is not a Mongoose House in Cambodia that shelters human trafficking survivors. But the idea for the place is based off real safe houses run by the Somaly Mam foundation and others by the Love146 non-profit. Both of these organizations were major inspirations for this story.

Boupha Mam is very much based off the real-life Somaly Mam. I've added a link to her organization and her book, *The Road of Lost Innocence,* at the end of this author note. Her story is a powerful one.

My long-term goal is to write one novella each year that tackles a different aspect of modern slavery. I'm calling this the *Freedom Series.* Some characters will overlap in this ongoing series, but for the most part each story will be a stand-alone novella.

When discussing human trafficking with others, some of the questions I'm often asked are, "What can I do? Is there really anything I can do that will make a difference?"

The answer is a resounding, "Yes!" You can help, and every effort makes a difference. To be clear, I'm not an expert and I don't work full-time in this worthy cause. In fact, I've had TV stations, newspaper reporters, and magazines ask me for interviews since they believed I was an "expert" about human trafficking. Every time I get these requests, I graciously tell them, "No, thank you," and direct them to the real experts working for the anti-trafficking NGO's.

I may not be an expert, but I try to do my own small part and I invite you to do the same. If you're wondering where to start, here is my shortlist of ways you can help.

1. Choose an NGO (non-profit) to support with monetary donations, volunteer hours, and be sure to share their posts on social media. Here are some of the NGO's I recommend.

o The International Justice Mission -
www.ijm.org
o Love146 - www.love146.org
o Free the Slaves - www.freetheslaves.net
o Not For Sale -
www.notforsalecampaign.org
o Somaly Mam Foundation -
www.somaly.org
o Operation Underground Railroad -
www.ourrescue.org

2. Study. Below is a suggested reading list to help you get informed.

o *Ending Slavery*, by Kevin Bales
o *The Road of Lost Innocence*, by Somaly Mam
o *Not For Sale,* by David Batstone
o *The Slave Next Door: Human Trafficking and Slavery in America,* by Kevin Bales

3. Sign petitions on Change.org in their Human Trafficking section. There are a mix of petitions to government and business leaders that aim to change laws and business policies dealing with aspects of human trafficking.
www.change.org/topics/humantrafficking#today

4. Going back to donations, I invite you to use www.smile.amazon.com whenever you shop on Amazon.com. This is Amazon's charitable donation site. It's exactly like Amazon.com (with the same prices and layout), but a percentage of all your orders are donated to the charity of your choice. If you're

like me and spend a lot on Amazon.com, the donations really start to add up.

Thank you again for reading *30 Red Dresses*. I hope you enjoyed the story and I invite you to get involved and make a difference in combating modern slavery.

All the best,
Johan Twiss

BOOK CLUB DISCUSSION
(From the author, Johan Twiss)

1. How did you experience the book? Were you immediately drawn into the story? Did the opening turn you away, or nearly turn you away from the book?

2. Did the book change your opinions or perspectives on modern slavery? Do you feel different now than you did before you read it?

3. Which character did you relate to the most, and what was it about them that you connected with?

4. What made the setting unique or important? Could the story have taken place anywhere?

5. Discuss the main **characters**—personality traits, motivations, and dynamics with one another.
- Veata and Chemsi
- Chemsi and Munny
- Munny and James
- James and Boupha
- Boupha and Veata
- Veata and James

6. What character growth or changes did you see over the course of the story?

7. Can you pick out a passage that really struck a chord with you?

8. What themes and symbolism did you find in the story?

9. If the book were being adapted into a movie, who would you want to see play what parts?

10. How did you feel about the ending?

11. Have you read any other books that I've written? (If not, feel free to grab them on Amazon.com :) Can you discern a similarity—in theme, writing style—between them? Or are they completely different?

12. If you were to talk with me (the author), what would you want to know? (see below)

CONTACT ME:
Feel free to contact me and ask your questions. Seriously, I'd love to talk with your book club via video chat or email. Just shoot me an email via my contact page at www.johantwiss.com/contact.html.

Thanks again for reading and I'd love to hear from you and/or participate with your book club. And if you enjoyed the story, leaving an honest review (and it can be a short 1-2 sentence review) on Amazon.com and Goodreads would mean the world to me.

All the best,
Johan

ACKNOWLEDGEMENTS

This book was a true labor of love and it would not be available without the help of some wonderful people. I want to thank my wife, Adrienne, for her support as my editor on this project and for her listening ear.

Thank you to my wonderful writing group in Dallas, Texas. One of my favorite times of the week is getting together for our late night critiques in the cafe at Barnes & Noble. Granted, a part of that is because they have great cheesecake. But y'all are a close second to the cheesecake.

Lastly, a huge thanks to all of the wonderful Beta Readers who took time to read and critique this story. Thank you Nuha Said, Wendy Basso, Lynn Parsons, Nicholas Burress, Kristin Ammerman, Candy Robosky, Rhonda Hampton, Jen Johnson, and Devora Burger. Your feedback helped improve the story and took it to the next level. Thank you!

JOIN THE CLUB!

Go to www.johantwiss.com to join the club today!

ABOUT THE AUTHOR

Dear Brilliant Reader,

Thank you for your interest in my books and I hope you enjoyed reading *30 Red Dresses*.

Have a question? Complaint? Want to send me suitcases full of money in small denominations or a gift card to the Cheesecake Factory? Simply reach out to me at my website, Facebook, or Twitter pages.

www.johantwiss.com
www.facebook.com/JohanTwiss
www.twitter.com/JohanTwiss

If you're part of a book club, I'd love to talk with your book club via video chat or email. You can reach me via my contact page at www.johantwiss.com/contact.html.

Lastly, I want to ask you for a favor. If you enjoyed reading this book, **please leave a review for it on Amazon.com**. Your reviews help new readers discover my books, for which I am thankful.

All the best,
Johan

(It's pronounced Yo-Han. Just pretend you saw Han Solo on Tatooine and said, "Yo, Han, what's up?")

OTHER BOOKS BY JOHAN TWISS

I AM SLEEPLESS: Sim 299

I AM SLEEPLESS: The Huntress

4 Years Trapped in My Mind Palace

The Fourth Law of Kanaloa

30 Red Dresses

Made in the USA
Columbia, SC
30 March 2019